GUY PSYCHO AND THE ZIGGURAT OF SHAME

★

John King

Published 2018 by Beating Windward Press LLC

For contact information, please visit:
www.BeatingWindward.com

Text Copyright © John King, 2018
All Rights Reserved
Author Photo by James King

First Edition
ISBN: 978-1-940761-39-8

Table of Contents

Personnel

Guy Psycho, *vocals*
Aleister Wrong, *guitars*
Lorrie Arkitron, *synths*
Philippe Grandeur, *bass*
Blee Gorgon, *percussion*

<u>*The Postmodernaires*</u>

Alexis
Aurora
Concetta
Daphne
Lulu
Matta
Pasha
Simone
Sybil
Tania
Trudy
Vernita

Style *is* meaning.

Chapter 1:
There is no Equilibrium

An immense rectangle of pulsating chrome squiggled up the mountain. Tires splashed across runoff from the exposed terrain, the firs clinging for life to the weeping rocks. From the rear of the bus, eight valves whooshed out nothing but the crispest, coolest oxygen into the piney air.

Inside the bus (in a soundproof chamber (in an ergonomic, translucent blue seat)) sat Archibald Fitzpatrick, C.P.A., the new manager of Guy Psycho and the Postmodernaires. He scratched his short, curly brown hair, leaned forward, his blue rep tie hanging at an angle. "Damn!" he thought.

Along the wall, silent screens ran in an omniscient matrix. One screen foretold the weather from Georgia to Chicago to Cairo. Another scrolled with financial tickers from New York, London, and Tokyo. Two *different* rugby scrims. Sumo wrestling. Several Busby Berkeley films, Fred Astaire's cheekbones immaculate and ghostly. And amongst the art deco kaleidoscopes of BB's choreography was footage from the band in Las Vegas. The chorus girls high-kicking, the musicians thrashing, and Guy Psycho crooning into antiquarian chrome. Every single camera angle was laced with bubbles. The silent footage was spooky, glamorous. Cool velvet and sequins. The harmonies of the Postmodernaires could sympathetically affect the vocal chords of anyone in a venue, or someone sitting by himself on a tour bus without the sound even being on.

Archibald's email was choked with messages from liquor companies, fashion houses, perfumeries, and the Las Vegas Chamber of Commerce to sponsor this tour. The computers in front of his bloodshot blue eyes were constantly getting strange messages in several languages. The internet was intermittent, a stream of interruptions. His coffee tilted in his stainless-steel mug.

Hired two weeks ago in a job interview that resembled a decadent kidnapping, Archibald thought he could make a difference in managing their assets and their business. He wasn't a show business accountant, which was among his chief attractions, apparently. But Archibald was having doubts.

They didn't have the credit to outlast the week.

Their expenditures strained comprehension: champagne pyramids, gratuitous couture, no thrift whatsoever when it comes to food—and who's buying all this sodium pentothal? And the weird venues were not helping. Why not a residency in Vegas, and why the hell *not* accept some of these sponsors, at least for the products they consume in such orgiastic quantities? The Sabre Room ought to have to wait. A surprise gig at the right clubs in Chicago or Nashville could take care of their banks for now. Archibald sat cool, statuesque, the cut of his Colin McFeeny trousers making him feel sharp. He printed out a data summary. He slipped on his jacket, which felt like an unconscious extension of his skin, like a slight tingling.

Opening the door may have been a mistake. Ninety decibels! Shimmering bubbles levitated thither and hither amidst strobes of heavenly disco-light, while twelve divine chorus girls, the Postmodernaires, jitterbugged. The gloopy pulsations of sound conformed to the undulations of the great bus. The angelic sway of bow-waisted cocktail dresses of scarlet satin and feminine flesh transfigured the fluttery air into a shadowy bacchanal of light. There was a manic vamping of Mary Janes on sparkling blue tile, and every seventh measure found oh so precise synchronic moments of their anatomical gestures in the Big, Bad Beat, no matter how the floor teetered with the bus's motions up the mountain. Archibald felt the mad beat vibrating through the soles of his tasseled loafers. All the Postmodernaires looked distinct from one another, each a unique physiognomy, but he couldn't yet tell them apart. Their images formed retinal afterthoughts, his pupils swelling into his blue irises, the most beautiful confusion in the world, as he gripped the wall for support.

Nearby, the four musicians of the Guy Psycho band sat stock-still. Each had black goggles on, looking down at rows of little beige squares. Archibald, his report in his hand, marveled at them, as they observed a hiatus in what *must* be another high-stakes game of Scrabble.

Blee Gorgon (drummer) stroked his purple soul-patch, wondering how he could make *something* of $C_3I_1G_2E_1M_3E_1U_1$ attempt a western conquest of the board, since the eastern side was congested, but couldn't conjure up anything more than U_1G_2, his U_1 a potential phalanx from the G_2 in $G_2R_1Y_4P_3H_4O_1N_1$.

Aleister Wrong (guitarist) was sweating, trickles oozing down the serpentine scar on his neck. Getting trounced. The entirety of Aleister's adult life had more or less been a succession of bad ideas, dating even further back than the Barbaric Yawp of the 1980s, back when he and Guy Psycho had enchanted thousands of juvenile delinquents. Or hundreds. Hardcore. This Scrabble match was stoopid. He couldn't spell. His mental lexicon slithered from his pores like sweat. For the Sabre Room show he was going to have to wash her clothes and play the rotten gig for free.

Lorrie Arkitron (keyboardist) started the game by locking the letters of $T_1Y_4P_3H_4O_1I_1D_2$ onto the grid, then moved later with $P_3O_1E_1S_1Y_4$ and *couped* her bandmates with a triple-word-scored $G_2R_1Y_4P_3H_4O_1N_1$. She smiled, two parentheses pulled down over her etched cheekbones, her blue lips pertly puffed out. The spires of her glittering hair cast minute shadows over her tiles, reflected in her black goggles. Untouchable.

And Philippe Grandeur (bassist) was zonked, an emanation of beatific drool sliming its way down his black vinyl jacket. The entire apparatus of self was immune to the extrasensory hints for a next move sent to him from Lulu (PhD, Philosophy, Yale, 2001; MA, Archeology, U of Chicago), the singular Postmodernaire who could best anyone on the bus at this game, should she elect to play (which she wouldn't, if she could be dancing (or reading (or eating those double-decker pink cupcakes from Old Hats)), although she kept one dreamy brown pupil affixed on that far off game, on that dreamy Frenchman). Philipe was in his own radiant heaven of solipsism, a mind of little ultrasonic booms.

Archibald climbed from the recreation area up through the bunkroom corridor to the end of the bus. He knocked on the black star, and stepped inside.

Blissful silence.

The Man had his back to Archibald, and stood before a round mirror rimmed with misty light bulbs. The whitest strip of gauze (Gaultier) was being wound, wound, wound into place around a very large neck, insulation for the vocal inflector that was installed after Guy Psycho contracted the Big C in his big throat.

(This unique biotechnological doodad (designed by the late Dr. Mapsichord) enables the Man to croon and talk in a natural-sounding voice—the torch-song voice, more or less, that he had acquired in the sanitarium, in the late cusp of the 1990s. The vocal inflector, though, is imperfect, and when it cannot overcompensate for the missing membranes in the Man's pipes, the timbre of his voice becomes a synthetic warble (like a vocoder, only prettier). When Dr. M took an errant mallet to the frontal lobe on the most pristine polo fields of Palm Beach, all hope of perfecting this marvel of plastic machinery died with him. Technicians from the doctor's estate do their best with monthly adjustments.)

A fastening pin (Gaultier) secured the end of the strip of cotton. Overlarge fingers pulled the collar of a midnight blue shirt close around the bandages, then twisted a few filaments from the top of a large, round head. Guy turned. The irises of his eyes were bejeweled with a glinting mixture of blue and green highlights, but always a little eerily fringed by the darkness of the black eye shadow of his eyelids, which looked like little holes when he blinked. The black lipstick, a dissonant, benevolent smile.

"Hello, Arch," said Guy, "Is your whis[tle] moist?"*

"Mr. Psycho," said Archibald, "We need to talk about the books."

"Rob[ert]o Bolaño?"

"Spreadsheets of our financials."

"Alas and crap," Guy said. "Yes. Very well, let's go [grab] ourselves a drink and chat all a[bout] it."

Archibald tried to suppress a wince. "Couldn't we discuss it in here, where it is quiet?"

Guy swung open the door and he and Arch stalked through the sleep-quarters.

"This is actually serious," Archibald said, "and just a little bit technical, so—"

They emerged into the recreation area, where the lights were now subdued, and a swinging version of

---

Apologetic editorial note: the occasional synthetic inflections of Guy's voice shall be punctuated by brackets.

Tennessee Waltz soughed from transparent speakers. Beneath a star-flare sconce, Lulu perused Adorno's *Studies in Husserl and the Phenomenological Antinomies*. Another Postmodernaire, Simone, was illuminated beneath another sconce, flipping through *Dioramas of the Inquisition*. Philippe had not shifted as much as a molecule from before. Everyone else was gone.

Guy zoomed to the bar. He grabbed an ice grinder, fed ice squares into the top, and then cranked the little handle with his very large hands. Icy shards were frayed into two tumblers. Guy then poured Zacapa rum into them, letting the brownness just barely lift the slivers. Archibald found a short crystal glass in his own uplifted hand. The topmost layer tilted ten degrees in the glass, according to the gradient of I-24. A spicy, honeyed fragrance prickled his nostrils.

"Mr. Psycho—"

When Archibald lifted his glass, he saw his employer had already downed his own drink.

"Call me Guy, Arch, I [in]sist."

"All right, Guy. I have something serious and quite important and rather freaking crucially, critically consequential to tell you."

"Are you *sure* you are[n't] going to drink [that]?"

"Quite."

Guy gazed at him with his greenish-blue eyes, which twinkled from the black crescents of his lids. He plucked the tumbler from Archibald's hand, and took a long sip from it.

"Do you have any idea how much money we are making?" Archibald asked.

"You mean [net] rather than gross?"

"Yes," said Archibald.

"Not the foggiest."

Archibald crumbled the paper in his fist.

"Guy, I don't think the Sabre Room is a good idea right now. We need bigger venues, or to go back to Nevada for more upscale showcases. We are—"

"As top as [not], don't [you] worry."

"Mr.—Guy—you hired me to keep this organization financially secure after the last 'manager' found himself on the wrong side of the law in Paraguay. You selected me because of my 'conscientious and pragmatic accounting experience.'"

"And because you look smashing in a dinner jacket. Please, I implore you, never do that air quotes thing again."

"Whyever did you spend $4,000 on this suit? It's not *me* that's on the stage."

"All the world's a stage, Arch, [all] the world's a cuckoo sta[ge]."

"Look, chief," Archibald said, and Guy's black lips formed a smile, "our expenditures are *un*sustainable. This technological Frankenstein of a bus, the fashion, the linens, the entrees, and my God, Guy, the avalanche of alcohol."

"Never say *avalanche* in the mountains. You *need* one [of] these," Guy said, materializing another tumbler into Archibald's hand.

"I am lowering the cap on all plastic—no casual spending over a thousand dollars," Arch said, slurping down rum before he realized what he was doing.

"Fair enough."

"And our credit cards will not authorize any purchases what-so-ever to liquor stores."

"You can't [do th]at, doobah."

"You'll find that I can, and that I already have. The Power of Attorney is in my contract."

"Look, I agreed [to] the cap, and—wait, you have [pow]er of attorney?"

"We spoke about this when you hired me."

"When was that?"

"Last month. The Manhattan Hilton?"

"And [I]—?"

"Yes."

"And I—?"

"Indeed, that too."

"Oh, [come] on, doobah!"

"I won't budge until we land a more lucrative gig."

"Are you out of your fffffff[fff]—"

The bus stalled. Guy opened the door and rushed through Archibald's office until he got to the front of the bus. Joseph Boovely, the driver, wasn't there. The door was open, letting in the tang of pine needles and late afternoon sunshine. Guy clattered down the steps, with Archibald close behind. They heard a litany of swearing from behind the bus. A siren goddess tattoo on a hand opened the engine hatch.

"What happen[ed]?" Guy asked.

"Precisely what I told you would happen," said Boovely, peering into the bland darkness of the engine. "This is too much bus for fuel cells, no matter how many cells you try to use."

"Don't be a pessimist. Can [you] fix it?"

"We need a flux capacitor to run this damn thing."

"Come now," said Guy, pursing his cheeks, and imploring him with kohl eyes. "We'll get one in [Chic]ago, but for now, *do* [some]thing magical."

"This is a bad idea. My guess is that the proton exchanges aren't wet enough, but to find out I am going to have to go through the stacks and plates. To get at our replacement parts, we're going to have to fork the Bubble Forge 8000 out of storage."

"What's the guestimated del[ay]?"

"Two hours? Six? It's going to get dark soon. We should sleep here and wait until morning light."

Archibald gritted his teeth.

"But, Joe," Guy said, "we *must* be in B[ig] Windy [by] tomorrow night."

"If we were diesel, we'd be there tonight. Even if I fix this thing, there's nothing to say that the identical problem won't happen again."

"I promise it won't."

"They didn't lobotomize you at St. Dymphna's?"

"Doesn't even leave a sc[ar] anymore, Boovie."

"I knew you would say that."

"S. M. G. O.," said Guy, kissing Joe's forehead.

"Yes, show must go on, Guy. I'll wake Wog and Wonk and set them at the bubbler."

"Capital. Where are we?"

"We are just outside Rock City."

"Detroit?"

"No, you baboon—Georgia's Rock City."

"Ah: so."

"There is a spot ahead where you can see seven states. Just follow the signs."

"That means se[ven] states will be able] to see *me*!"

"Idiot," muttered Simone.

"Should we be scooching off without bodyguards, Guy?" asked Archibald.

Wog and Wonk were bald gladiators, whose massive bulks needed little more than an arched eyebrow to make even the crunkest audience member, intrusive paparazzi, or anyone else act like civilized people. The musculature of their torsos was tectonic, strapped with black spandex polo shirts. Their upper arms were impossibly huge swerves of meat and muscle with veins the size of garden hoses. Their necks swelled out of the spread collars of their shirts. Their heads looked as hard and unforgiving as their muscles. Their long black Slavic eyebrows warped up into their foreheads. When they needed to do more than arch an eyebrow, the results were irrecoverable, and done without emotion. They didn't even *like* music. They were perfect machines. Loyal to Guy.

"What [harm] could come?" Guy said, contemplating the mountain scenery. "Besides, the show must go [on]. They are needed [more] where they are."

Archibald watched as the two Atlases lifted out the silver engine of the Bubble Forge 8000 and eased it to ground on the shoulder of asphalt. Then Wog tossed steel suitcases to Wonk, who lined them up like dominos. Two dozen, three dozen, taking on the reddish-brown tint of the mountain walls. Joe then walked cursing into the storage chambers underneath the bus with an illuminated visor. Wog and Wonk stood watching over the bus, over the gear, over the highway, in readiness for everything and nothing.

Archibald didn't like this. He wanted to call everyone back, to stay together with the bus. But when he looked down the road, the line of their people stretched a half-mile, with Guy dancing in the lead. He took selfies of himself with his long, outstretched arm. He was already so far away.

Chapter 2:
A Chance Meeting

Archibald pinched a rock from his loafer. He tested his reception: nil bars.

They marched in an opulent processional along asphalt inclines. The clacking of Mary Janes upon the shoulder of I-24 sounded like a herd of deer. As the light mellowed through the pines towards dusk, Lulu pulled a leather jacket close to her torso to keep out the slight chill. After what seemed like miles, the quaint, persistent "SEE ROCK CITY" signs at long last led them to a darkening, woodsy empty parking lot.

Near a gigantic red birdhouse, which overlooked a bed of trumpet lilies and bloomy azaleas, a thirty-five-foot limousine idled. Its polished blackness reflected all eighteen people, with a slight warping of perspective where the tinted windows stretched from the sleek, dark frame.

"Would you look at that," said Trudy, popping her bubble gum. She gazed at her round face, beautifully distended in the convexity of the rearview mirror.

The group of posh hikers clambered up the steps to the long country house that served as the entrance to the park. Guy flung open the French doors, clanging upon the walls, sashes shivering. Behind the counter, the woman in a tweed dress smiled. "The Park closes soon," she murmured in response to Guy's raised eyebrow, as everyone else congealed around him.

"Very well," he said, "Eighteen tickets, ple[ase]."

"Oh, never mind. Go on up, just kindly come back before 8 o'clock."

"Thank you large," said Guy.

"You *are* going to behave yourselves, aren't you?" the woman asked.

"We [are] docility incarnate."

"Mm-hmmm. Well, you won't wants to be late for your prom."

"Posilutely," said Simone, her long, blonde hair turning in her wake.

"Watch out for snakes," said the woman as they shuffled out the other side.

The Postmodernaires harmonized,
> "Echo, echo, everywhere we go
> Life is a game that's played on the run
> If there's some vinyl that can be spun
> Spin it with Bim-bam-bummm
> Bim-bam-bummm
> Hit that drum,"

as they clacked up the mountain steps with careless, little Rockette kicks. The remainder of the company trailed them.

"If there isn't some icy vodka at the top of this hill, I'll throw myself off it," groused Aleister.

"Chins up, fiends," cheered Guy, "this [is] some sublime, magisterial, dangerous scenery, so enjoy it, and Joe w[ill] pick us up in the parking lot. Now breathe in God's grandeur before I st[omp] the snot out of you."

Philippe cackled to himself.

Archibald wished he had some more iced rum.

And Trudy performed a perfect pirouette at the top of the flag court, where the various nationalities hung before a violet gray sky. Land and gravity peeled away from the world, as if the mountains had been waiting an eternity to be entertained, or perhaps it was the other way around. Guy hopped onto the railing. "Oh, the view is terr[if]," he said. "Like a spectrograph of geography."

"Sweetie, please don't," intoned Matta.

"Yeah," said Blee, "you're blocking the mountain!"

Guy smacked the tips of his fingers to his blackened lips, and then popped down.

"Can we see Lover's Leap next?" gushed Aurora.

"Well," said Guy, "what o'clock is [it]?"

"Seven forty-six," said a voice behind them. "Not much time, if you ask me."

The man had a wiry physique, and wore a belted flannel suit that hasn't been in style since the 1940s. His rakish dark hair was brylcreemed close to his scalp, and a thin, neat layer of peppery stubble lined the man's beard. He set the ivory tip of a cigarette holder between his perfect, white teeth, and then fastened a Turkish brand into the outer end. Then he pulled a mother-of-pearl lighter from a fob pocket and emitted a long, thin flame to ignite the smoke. He exhaled with a sighing sangfroid.

"How do you do?" asked Guy.

"Everything," said the stranger. "And perhaps you do, too, Mr. Psycho."

"I certainly [used] to," said Guy. "Might I have the pleasure of [know]ing who *you* rather [are]?"

"Youngerman, Taylor Charles Edward," he said with a locked jaw, "but please just call me T. C. E."

"You don't have a Georgia accent," noted Lorrie.

"I live nearby, in Tennessee. But my family has never acquired the local dialect."

"Say, that's *your* car outside, isn't it?" asked Pasha.

"Oh, yes," said T. C. E.

"Your family has been in the mountains awhile?"

"Who are you?"

"Archibald Fitzpatrick, the business manager."

"Five generations," said T. C. E., mesmerized by the diamond earrings of the Postmodernaires sparkling in the dying dusk light, like fireflies, so that he ignored Archibald's existence.

"Well, *ciao*, baby," said Guy. "Let's moose, [you] cats, and not upset the nice lady."

"Wait a moment," said T. C. E.

Guy breathed so deeply that his dinner jacket swelled up and nearly popped a $400 button—and then let the breath out.

"That was precisely [one] moment," he said, turning to leave.

"One more moment, please," said T. C. E., a touch of ire in his voice.

"Hey, now, I only ha[ve so] many moments."

"Where are you supposed to be?" Youngerman asked.

"Chicago, tomorrow night."

"My wife and my son are very fond of your work."

"Thank them [large]."

"Why don't you thank them yourself?"

"Hm[mm]?"

"Why not come to my house?"

"Well—"

"I would like you to play for us tomorrow morning."

"That really [isn't] possible."

"Everything is always possible."

"True though that [may] be, it doesn't apply to you, and it does not apply to [now]. There are some [very] hip, very [loy]al people up there that—"

"You need not disappoint them."

"I cannot set up two [shows] in that time, and there is no venue here."

"There is a stage at my home that believe it or not Sammy Davis, Jr. once found more than adequate."

"But the technical equipment [there can]not—"

"—it is state of the art."

"But we shall require bubbles, and our [mach]ine is back in our bus."

"Which is broken down. And I can hire, at a moment's notice, a hundred enthusiastic children who would be more than eager to blow out bubbles for the duration of your performance."

"Weird."

"Really?" asked T. C. E. scribbling onto a pad.

"Perhaps not," Guy sneered, his black mouth warping.

"Look, Mr. Psycho, it is important that you do this."

Archibald stepped between the two men, cupped his hand to Guy's ear, and whispered: "Listen to his offer: There will be *no* booze in Chicago if you don't at least listen."

"Do you realize what [you] are saying?"

"Perfectly."

"Are you drunk?"

"Not yet. Either *you* listen to his offer, or else you live dry well into next week."

"You're turning in[to] a pest, cricket," said Guy. He turned to Mr. Youngerman and said, "Mr. Younger[man], while we appreciate your good will and [enth]usiasm, this merry band of ours live [and] work according to certain moral [and] aesthetic protocols. I am sorry, but we do not perform private [e]vents at any price."

The man upheld a check written out for FIVE MILLION DOLLARS.

"—except that one, doobah," Guy added, the whites of his eyes blooming large. "And *only* if you agree [to] all seventy-seven riders."

"Certainly," said T. C. E. Youngerman.

"Arch, do you have our contract?"

"Right here, chief!"

"Zippity-zing!" said Trudy.

Chapter 3:
What the Basement Saw

Archibald Fitzpatrick squatted on the stretch limousine's floor. He adjusted his blue rep tie, trying not to appear to gaze up the Postmodernaires' dresses, or to stare too long at their dancer's legs, although their Chanel no. 12 distracted him. He was also trying not to be stepped on by the musicians, whose bodies arose up around him through the sunroof, as they conducted some sort of conversation screamed through the wind. The inchoate murmuring above made eavesdropping on Mr. Youngerman and Guy almost impossible. A pain pierced his frontal lobe.

Guy, however, seemed to be behaving, sitting with his elbows on his knees, inclining his pale, dark form towards Mr. Youngerman, locked in an amiable conversation. The Postmodernaires sipped their martinis and chattered to themselves, ranking various glee clubs that Archibald had never heard of, or could even conceive of, dating back to the 1950s. Then they discussed the newest song in their repertoire, "This Eve With No Tomorrow," and whether Lorrie Arkitron's avant-garde choreography for the up-tempo tune revealed sadistic impulses. Mostly sadistic, the consensus was.

And then the girls went mum as the long, black vehicle came through the craggy woods and the Youngerman estate seem expanded before them like a mass mirage—a five-story outgrowth of the mountain itself, dwarfing the whirring pines. The effect was as if someone had designed a lean-to as a rustic palace. A mansard roof slanted a hundred feet from the mountainside. The front of the house was green and striated with slate, punctured here and there with what looked like little illuminated windows that grew larger as they approached. A woman stalked a balcony high above, her dress airy. The bottom of the house's structure featured the thick glass walls of a rotunda rather than a stone exterior. Above the sunroof, the musicians applauded this spectacle, the reflection of this mad architecture enlarging in the lenses of their shades, while below them the Postmodernaires soon clamored close to the window to see this hallucination better. Guy and T. C. E. never looked up from their private conversation, whatever it was about.

The car stopped, and the PMs poured out, fresh martinis aloft, and the band and Guy and Archibald filtered into the whispering of the evening around them. English Ivy strangled its way up a mosaic of limestone shapes, twisting around the open squares from which dun-colored curtains undulated in the slightness of breeze.

"Everyone inside," warbled Mr. Youngerman, "the night is wasting. You have a show to perform."

The sloping marbled stairs up to the front verandah made the approach so gradual that the guests forgot the tectonic enormity of the house. Inside, however, the long gallery of the vestibule led to a huge rotunda. Through the glassy dome overhead, the low moon looked like an olive in the world's largest cocktail. Before their feet, a mosaic appeared in the form of a crest, with a swan ascendant, over quills and arrows. From the mosaic, a staircase curved into the space, Mary Jane heels clicking on glass. At the upper level, a man with a red Van Dyke beard, in a black tailcoat, waited with pristine patience.

"Everyone," Mr. Youngerman said, "before supper, I suspect you'll want to freshen up? Change your clothes? Reginald here will escort you to some quarters where you can do so. Dinner will be served in an hour."

"Might we have a tour of your home?" asked Trudy.

"After dinner," said T. C. E., "you shall see to your heart's content."

Archibald paced across the dark wooden floor. In his left hand, he swung the base of the heavy black telephone (an antique, circa 1964), as he upheld the receiver to the side of his face. He was trying to get both Guy's own private banker and Mr. Youngerman's bank president into a conference call, to ensure that Mr. Youngerman's check was kosher, even though Youngerman's house seemed like evidence enough. Archibald paced. He had been on the job less than two weeks, and this was a sign that he was doing good things. Righting the craft. He was not even dividing to see what his own share of this profit would be—he was so focused on verifying that this was indeed a go.

A valet requested that he stand still, and as soon as Archibald put his heels together, the valet brushed down his black McFeeny suit. Mr. Youngerman's bank president was being paged in an undisclosed corner in Vale, in some sort of secretive telephonic relay. Archibald heard Philippe showering somewhere, a raspy baritone bawling out *Toujours Aimer* with exquisite echoes splattering with the force and purity of a secret mountain stream. The Postmodernaires refreshed themselves in some other wing of the mansion. The rest of the band slouched upon a round, zebra-skin bench with sundry highballs in their upraised hands. Lorrie's blue concoction was garnished with the miniature tentacle of some unimaginable creature. Another valet trimmed Blee's soul-patch, small scissors glinting around that tiny purple peninsula on his chin. *Snap-snap.* Archibald gazed downward: his valet had burnished his loafers until the light-tips of the chandelier reflected in the leather.

"Dinner is served," said Reginald.

"This is Mr. Ansler," said a voice on the telephone receiver, and Archibald knew that he would be late to dinner. He looked into a huge, gilt mirror: did the valet just trim his brown curls?

"If Tommy D jazzed up [the] Voice, and Gordon Jenkins taught the instr[u]ments to make love to th[at] song," said Guy, sipping from a sliver of *Vin Fin De la Cotes De Nuits* 1957, "then it was Nelson Riddle hims[e]lf who finally put the Sin [in] Sinatra."

An interminable table flickered beneath a forest of candlesticks.

"Then what was Quincy Jones?" asked Trish Youngerman, incurving her spoon into some pheasant mousse. A pink pump churned along the chalk-stripes of Guy's calf.

"The translator who made B[a]sie into a cocktail to drown in."

"What are you talking about?" asked Archibald, as he wedged a chair between Lorrie Arkitron and Lulu. Lulu, like the other Postmodernaires, had taken the opportunity in the hour before the dinner and to change clothes from the guest wardrobes. She wore a short dress, aswirl with Modern modular shapes, and a black polo with a zippered-closure for the collar. She also wore, in the chill of the huge room a sleek black leather jacket and tapped the floor with clunky motorcycle boots. Archibald noticed that Lulu had noticed that he was looking at her leg as it smoothed out of the black leather, so he stared at his own miniature, concave reflection in his burnished spoon.

"So?" Edwin Youngerman asked the group. He was a younger clone of his father, muscular and thin, hair gelled down, but taller, clean-shaven, and in a houndstooth suit. "Who is your favorite Beatle?"

"Pete Best," said Blee.

"Definitely R[ingo]," murmured Guy.

"I favor the Blue Meanies," smarmed Aleister.

"Shall you perform your Goth version of 'Windmills of Your Mind?' for us tomorrow?" asked Trish, licking the end of her glistening spoon.

"We can *certainly* accommodate that," said Archibald.

"Mr. Psycho, was the arrangement for that something you thought up in St. Dymphna's?" asked Youngerman the Younger.

Guy blinked blackly at him, his blue-green irises a vacuum, and his large fingers poked against his temples. One hand then reached down and smoothed the bandage around his neck, the whole time his eyes not shifting, and always, always blinking.

"N[o]," Guy said, before a long draught of pinot grigio.

"When will we get our tour?" Simone asked in T. C. E.'s direction.

"Precisely now," said T. C. E., "let me shew you around." To his wife, he said, "If you'll excuse us, my dear," and she clattered her spoon onto the china. Her shoe-tip grazed Guy's knee as he arose.

Mr. Youngerman presented the theater, a huge space several stories tall. The walls protruded with meticulous Grecian scenes, pastoral misadventures of livestock and lovers, and the musical battle between Apollo and Dionysus. A chandelier radiated overhead like an anemone of light. Three overstuffed velvet chairs rested in the room's center. The front of the long, darkened stage was fringed with the clamshell housings for old-fashioned footlights.

"Can you acc[o]mmodate state-of-the-art technical [eq]uipment in *here?*" huffed Guy, a frown wrinkling his round face.

Reginald coughed behind them. There, against the back wall, was a huge sound-booth, with enough blipping lights for a NASA launch. A series of twelve earpiece microphones, each one labeled with a Postmodernaire's name, were arrayed on its counter-top.

Reginald activated a switch, and spotlights came onto the stage, as well as the footlights, in a rainbow of molten colors. On the stage an electric guitar, an electric bass, a drum kit, a grand piano, and a vintage chrome microphone awaited use.

"The stage is [wide], but not deep," Guy observed. "Lovelies, [do you] want to dance on the stage, or in front of the stage?"

"*In front,*" they sang in unison.

"You know," Lorrie said to Guy, "this space upholds your prejudice for historical venues."

"A [grand] piano is okay with you?" he asked.

"It's worked for other people, I suppose," Lorrie said.

"Sarah Bernhardt once portrayed Lear here, for my grandfather," said Mr. Youngerman.

"You mean she played Cordelia?" asked Lulu.

"No, *she* played Lear," said Youngerman, "as well as Gloucester, Edgard, Edmund, and Oswald. She was, I'm told, quite sublime, even with only one leg."

Despite the theater being on the second floor, its other tall doors opened into a garden—the maze of which Mr. Youngerman would under no circumstances allow his party to enter. Archibald felt a momentary twinge at the mysterious waivers that their host had added to the contract. At the time, Archibald was too pleased that their employer never balked at Guy's contractual demands, some of which were quite silly (no white shoes permitted among the audience, for example). As far as Mr. Youngerman was concerned, why would he think the band might destroy the garden grounds? It didn't seem plausible. But—if the house abutted a mountain, why couldn't they see the garden from outside, when they first arrived at the house?

Through the garden, they then entered the library, which also served as a smoking room. Club chairs squatted over the arabesques of the largest Arabian carpet any of them had ever seen. Wheeled ladders rose ten feet into the air. Little flames from the fireplace appeared in the glass cases of very antiquated books. The low molded ceiling gave the room a sense of intimacy the rest of the house did not with all its grandeur. Mr. Youngerman fixed a cigarette into the holder he clamped between his teeth.

"Have you anything rare?" asked Matta, dangling a signed first edition of *The Picture of Dorian Gray*. She smiled, showing off her sharp canines between red lips.

Mr. Youngerman took the tome away from her. "We have everything."

He showed her uncut, first editions of Eugene Sue, duodecimos of Phillip Sydney, the English edition proofs for *The Bell Jar*, even the Shakespeare and Co. first run of *Ulysses*. Pasha reached out a hesitant finger to the sacred blue leather of the last tome.

"Just words?" said Matta, sighing, twisting the hem of her diaphanous dress.

"Oh, much better than that."

"Show me," said Matta.

"Heh," he said, "aren't you the willful pumpkin. Follow me, then." He brought the band from another door in the library down a fusty corridor to a large red door. Removing a large, old-fashioned key from the waist-pocket of his gray flannel jacket, he twisted the lock and then ushered the party into a vaulted white room, lined by row after row of glass cases.

"Wowsa," said Matta, her silver go-go boots clacking with an echo. "You win!"

"We have almost one of every thingamabob, from Alexandria to Zanzibar. Look, here is a Welsh garderobe from the Dark Ages, with its ore still un-mined, rescued from an almost invisible gorge in the cliffs of Cardiff, by Sir Willoughby B. Willoughby, in 1877."

"Are you sure it's genuine?" asked Archibald.

"Carbon dating confirmed it."

"What's a garderobe, anyway?" asked Aurora, fluffing her feathery red hair. "And why would your ancestors move something so old all the way to Tennessee, for your own private collection?"

T. C. E. Youngerman smirked, gazing among the vast symmetrical lines of his great archeological dominion. *Here* there was a headdress that may have belonged to Cleopatra. *There* was Betsy Ross's thimble. And—over—there:

Indecipherable tablets,
    Mark Antony's plumed, golden helmet,
    A Quin Dynasty dragon in lapis lazuli,
    A generic brown crate (#9906753),
    A saxophone pawned by Charlie Parker,
    J. Edgar Hoover's lacy, lilac bra,
    A tapestry of Sir Gawain and the Green Knight,
    A Mason-jar of Moon dust,
    & W. Shakespeare's Stratford school desk.

The party swirled around these cases, consuming these items ripped from the past with their eyes, as if the images taunted their own audacity, as if history was babbling in its own still confinement. Lulu noticed the *whiz* of security cameras panning to watch every hair's breath movement of their limbs. As they spread out into this capacious chamber, each glassy shape held some new strange wonder. Guy was transfixed by an eight-foot tall demon's head mask from Africa that reminded him of his grandfather. Vernita, the tallest of the Postmodernaires, stared up at a statue of Venus, whose roseate cheeks seemed to defy Time. Nearby, Lorrie watched a cluster of shrunken heads as if they might make strain against their sewn lips, to confess unimaginable histories.

In the final row, in a very slender case, a pair of eroded Doc Martins reposed on a green cushion. A brass plaque read: "Guy Psycho, footwear, circa 1981."

"My wife picked those out," said Mr. Youngerman.

"Well, I suppose I *am* done w[i]th them," said Guy, looking down at the glinting wingtips on his feet.

"If your collection is still growing," asked Matta, "then what happens when you run out of space in this room?"

"Voila," said Mr. Youngerman, removing a remote control from his inside jacket pocket. He pointed the device at the whitewashed brick wall, and with a click, the wall groaned away from them, expanding the room's size. The wall kept disappearing further into the house, and the room yawned monstrously in an infinite regress.

"Soon enough, you'll have enough pieces here for a museumumumum," said Blee, his voice echoing into the gaping emptiness.

Squinting at them, Youngerman rubbed his peppery stubble, sleeked down his hair with his hand. "A museum?" he huffed. "A museum is nothing more than an anarchic vulgarium. Everything is connected by the firm fist of Destiny, but that fist is not in the clouds, it is our own," he boasted, flourishing his bony hand. "A museum has the soul of an amusement park. What this is, is history." He adjusted his scowl into a triumphant smirk. "I think you had better follow me," he said, "We haven't much time."

He stumped off a long way in front of them, until a passageway in the left wall became exposed about a hundred feet in. "Come come, the most exciting is over here," he said, and they followed him. The stone passageway he stood in front of led to a large service elevator. "Step in, please," said Mr. Youngerman.

He closed the gate.

The platform plummeted into the earth. The 100-watt bulb atop the elevator frame rendered them into silhouettes as they descended further and further into the black, as the winch squealed them stratum by stratum into the oblivion of the earth. Gradually, the whine of the cable arose in pitch, and everyone felt as if his or her masses were lightening. Wisps of the Postmodernaires' hair arose.

And then it stopped. Mr. Youngerman slid open the gate and escorted them down a stone corridor lit by gaslights: and then another, leading out onto a ledge with the faint outline of some sort of railing. He handed out flashlights to everyone in the party.

"Why have you dragged us down to this hole in the ground?" asked Lulu.

"To show you what no museum will ever have," said Youngerman, flicking an enormous switch on the wall. With a profound *zlurch*, a hundred floodlamps bathed a monolithic geometry, a sublime profusion of angles, in pristine light.

Chapter 4:
Ishtar's *Boudoir*

"What the cr[a]pola is that?" quizzed Guy, his black lids blinking.

On the shale floor far below them, an immense trapezoid of dappled masonry arose two hundred feet, sloping inward to a long, intricate terrace adorned with russet and golden hedges. From the center of that terrace, a smaller trapezoid of dappled masonry arose a hundred feet, sloping inward to a more intricate terrace adorned with russet and golden hedges: and from the center of *that* terrace, a smaller trapezoid even still arose, and so on and so on and so on until the walls at long last sloped inward to a single temple building. Before the entire structure, a vast stairway splayed in three dizzying directions, conjoined inside an angular turret atop the first terrace, forming a steep, singular ascent to the tip-top, to the temple.

"That," whispered Lulu, "is a ziggurat."

"I never did," said Guy.

"What?"

"I was [a]cquitted."

"I said *ziggurat*," said Lulu. "If His Royal Serrated Brain would condescend to focus—"

"Yes, *mon petit ch[a]t.*"

"Mr. Youngerman, you have a ziggurat in your basement."

"I do, don't I?" said Mr. Y, smiling so much his dimples emerged from his peppery stubble.

"It's enormous."

"The largest in the world—in fact, the largest in the *history* of the world."

"But how? When?"

"Yes."

"The reconstruction must have taken—"

"The find came over from Mesopotamia intact, actually, via my great-grandfather's steamer, the Nouveau Argosy."

"But this cavern," Lulu said, noting the lack of tonsilly stalactites and stalagmites, "your crews—"

Mr. Youngerman sighed.

"But how did your great-granddaddy squeeze an entire—" asked Lulu.

"They hefted it sideways through a crag in the mountain."

"*What* crag in the mountain?"

"Oh, we sealed that up long ago, my dear. Can't encourage thieves, you know."

"Sure," said Lulu, a glossy red smile wavering, glitter glistening on her cheekbones. The tableau in front of her, below her, was an affront, both philosophically and archeologically. The geometry of a ziggurat was to get the temple closer to heaven, so to have it underground—

Even if this were a hoax, the scale of the thing defied sanity, even considering how that term might be treated among the Postmodernaires. And if it weren't a hoax, her own father—

Meanwhile, the retinue clanked down, down, down a spiraling steel staircase until they stood twenty feet before the enormous structure.

"It's a pyramid," scoffed Aleister Wrong.

"No, it's a ziggurat," corrected Lulu.

"It's not a pyramid?"

"It's not a pyramid. It's a ziggurat."

"So it's not a pyramid?"

"Look—"

Philippe leaned into Aleister's nape and whispered into the guitarist's smashed auricle a moment. "Oh yeah," muttered Aleister, "what *is* a ziggurat?"

"I was getting to that," said Lulu, softening. "A ziggurat is, well, a Sumerian temple once found in ancient Mesopotamia. Later the region was known as Babylonia, and even later than that Assyria."

"So it's a Babylonian p[y]ramid?" asked Guy.

"No. Pyramids don't have stairs."

"Ah."

"And my guess, although this cannot be right, is that the edifice is ancient—too old to be Babylonian. Am I right, Mr. Y?"

"Your summary is admirably accurate, my dear. And quick. Your reputation is well-founded. Bravo."

"You know who I am?"

To which Mr. Youngerman offered a gray flannel shrug, a hereditary gesture inherited from very old Youngermans, a patronizing non-signifier almost as ancient as the treasures the family collected.

"This—this is the *oldest* ziggurat in existence?" Lulu asked.

"Oh, yes—of *known* existence, for those few who know it—like yourselves. History never dies, though it may slumber a very long time. And here my family has given it an ideal bed for dreaming. Shall we go up?"

"And w[a]ke up history?"

"Perhaps," said Mr. Youngerman.

"Very well, th[e]n," said Guy, "where['s] the escalator?"

Lulu's avid advance up the ancient mud-brick steps preempted any other words on that subject. Everyone hustled behind her. Guy stared at Mr. Youngerman as the old man passed him on the stairs. "Th[i]s was all part of your pl[a]n," he said.

Mr. Youngerman again offered an atavistic, inscrutable shrug.

"*Where* did this come from?" asked Lulu, her glossy lips worming in astonishment, the black circle of her irises flaring large despite the great whiteness of the floodlamps.

"East of the Euphrates, in the city of Uruk."

"But why has no one ever written—"

"Sir Richard Sutton Essex got there well before Loftus, and my grandfather's partner was, to say the least, discreet."

"It dates all the way back to the Uruk period, when the city reigned over the Sumerian people?"

"Alas, no. It is from a later period, when Uruk was declining. Essex himself believed the temple itself was hidden somehow."

"How?"

"We really don't know. Essex was shocked to have found it at all."

"What are [you] talking about?" asked Guy.

"Shush," said Lulu. "Is this Ishtar's temple, then?" she asked Mr. Youngerman.

"Certainly."

At the summit, Lulu looked down. The other Postmodernaires climbed with ease, while the musicians seemed to wheeze their way up, passing around Lulu and Mr. Youngerman. They stalked closer to the black rectangle of the temple passage.

"Shouldn't we be getting back," said Archibald, "getting ready for the show, or sleep, or whatever?"

Mr. Youngerman nudged a knob with his foot, and a little *zlurch* resounded from the opening. "Let's have a look," he said, and walked inside.

They entered a wide, indigo antechamber, with a

luminous pool of motionless water in its center. Blee Gorgon reached down a long finger to scratch its surface.

"Careful, young man," warned Mr. Youngerman, "That's the bathwater of a goddess."

"Holy water?"

"In a sense."

"Can I drink it, then?" asked Blee.

"I wouldn't, if I were you," said Mr. Youngerman.

"So then," said Lulu, "when you say this is Ishtar's temple, you meant *not* the place where she was worshipped, but rather—"

"Where her [very] own pad is," ventured Guy.

"In your words, yes," said Mr. Youngerman.

"Why isn't the water cold?" asked Blee.

Mr. Youngerman shrugged.

The group quietly moved from the pool chamber to the next room. The walls emanated heat. To the left and their right, passages revealed rooms with oversized wine casks, and small granaries of wheat and barley. That musty fragrance one associates with antiquity was missing. The indigo walls stretched, and then stopped with a narrow opening in the far wall. Strange geometric somethings appeared over the gap.

"What do those funny words say?" asked Simone, prodding Lulu in the side of her leather jacket.

"I don't know" said Lulu, "Why ask me? I don't really do languages other than English, French, Latin, Italian, and (sort of) German." But she was scrutinizing the peculiar characters nonetheless.

"Come on, Lulu!"

"I'm a philosopher, not a linguist."

"Remember last week when you said that Plato was a better demiurge than thinker?"

"The word is *dramaturge*."

"That proves you're the right woman for the job. Bee-sides, you studied archeology!"

"And I stopped before becoming an archeologist, in part, because I couldn't gear up dead languages. I just couldn't—and then there was all the Alexanders—"

"I know what it says," Guy interrupted.

"How can *you* know what it says?" said Lorrie, waving her electrified field of hair.

"I just [*do*], is all."

"What's it say, then?"

"'Do not [enter].'"

"Is he right?"

"As best I can make out, I *think* so," said Lulu, squinting.

"Yes, he's dead on," confirmed Mr. Youngerman.

"What do we do now?"

"There's on[ly one] thing *to* do," Guy said. He sauntered through the narrow threshold, and kept walking. The Postmodernaires, the band, and Archibald Fitzpatrick gazed at one another a moment, and then hastened after their boss, through the door.

Mr. Youngerman, his peppery whiskers distending in a smile, watched until the last of them squeezed through.

As they swelled out on the other side, a small cone of light emanated from a table along a sidewall. A fat leather journal lay open, and more cuneiform appeared on the left side of its pages, with English parallel to it on the right. Lorrie peered down.

"What's it say?" she asked.

"It says, 'Gilgamesh is—is a fink?'" said Lulu.

"Really?"

"Mm-hmm."

"Wasn't he the villain [o]n the Smurfs?" asked Guy.

"No," said Lulu.

"Oh."

"He's the hero of an epic."

"I [see]."

"Do you?"

"The people of his kingd[om] were weary of his b[ull]ish reign, and so the gods sent him [a] BFF, a cosmological equal to befuddle and befriend him."

"Enkidu."

"Doesn't r[o]ll off the tongue, does it?"

"My tongue rolls pretty—wait: so you were playing dumb all this time?"

"I [nev]er *play* dumb. But my memory [i]s—can be—fragile, my dear."

"Ah, yes."

"So where *are* we?"

"A dressing chamber," said Simone.

"How can you tell?"

Simone unfurled a diaphanous swirl of tunic in front of her body. From an opening of an ornate trunk, rings of golden wristbands lay curled. On an overlarge, gilded skull stood a wig of cascading layers of dark manes about four feet in length. A dazzling amulet with a bull figure, with diamonds for its eyes, lay on a chair. Simone tickled the surface of her skin with the fabric, a toothy, Cheshire smile on her face.

"How dreamy."

"I would set that down," murmured Lulu, "right pronto."

"Couldn't we just *try*—" asked Simone.

"Something," said Lulu, "strange is going on here."

"Stranger than normal?" asked Lorrie.

Archibald sighed.

"Mr. Youngerman might [not] have been joking about Ish[tar] *living* here."

"Is it even possible that you're serious?" asked Simone.

"No. It's not wh[at] I do. But I am [be]ginning to think that *he* was serious."

"What makes you say that?"

"Because he isn't here any[more]."

The great novelty of their surroundings had made them miss their host's absence.

"Yes," Guy said, interrupting the cacophony of gasping, "in his [own] batty way I would say Mr. Youngerman *is* [ver]y capable of being quite serious."

"Well, what do we do now?" asked Archibald.

"Here is the point where we should go back, and stop ourselves from getting any deeper," intoned Lorrie.

"*No, wait, come back*—that sort of thing?" asked Trudy.

"Yes."

But Lulu, leaning against the table, was engrossed with the leather journal in her lap. "There are transcriptions here," she said.

"Of what?" asked Alexis, tracing the lines of her blonde finger wave with her fingertips.

"Somewhere in this structure there are tablets of *Gilgamesh*. An alternate version."

"Which means what?"

"History is not always written by the victors."

"Which means, umm, what?"

"Which means someone has something to say about her own story, I think. That's why *this* is here."

"Which means what?"

"We've been sent here to jam with some very old mythology."

"But why?"

"Wh[y] not?" said Guy.

"But aren't you afraid Mr. Youngerman set us up?" asked Simone, the black tassels of her dress quivering.

"Do you think that Mr. Youngerman even intends to see the show, Guy?"

"He pays like [a] Philistine."

"Philistines were Egyptian," said Lulu.

"Slacken the [noose], won't you, darl[ing]?"

"*Oui, mon chat noire.*"

"So what are we going to do, boss?" asked Lorrie.

"Frank Sinatra n[ever] boozed with a goddess—did he (Ava [G.] notwithstanding)?"

Lorrie scowled.

"Mr. Fitzpatrick, what do *you* think?" asked Trudy.

"Have you ever heard of lemmings?" asked Archibald.

"Can't say that I [have]," said Guy.

"We ought to head back," said Archibald, scratching at the dust with the shiny toe of his loafer. "There is too much we don't know. For example, whose journal is that, and who is tending the garden on the lower terrace, and who is keeping the water clean, and stocking the storage rooms with all those provisions. There ought to be a lot of people around here, but I don't see any. And where the diabolical hell is Youngerman? We have no financial options should anything dangerously weird happen while we are here. This is not to mention the very real possibility that we could get, you know, sort of—"

"Zilched?"

"Yes. So let's return upstairs, get a miserable half-night's sleep, and then ready yourselves for the show at dawn."

"We can't do that," said Matta.

"Why not?" asked Archibald.

"Because that doorway we used is gone."

The entrance they had crept inside was now indeed a solid plane of indigo wall. Archibald patted his hand where the aperture had been, although he did so distractedly, as if part of his brain had already accepted the inevitability that there was no going back. Without gazing down at the chair, he took the amulet in his proprietary hands, shifted its weight to the table, and plopped down like a zombie, like a mummy, like a wearied C.P.A. He wished he were back on the broken-down bus. If the gang of them managed to escape this misadventure alive, he would earn 14% of six million dollars, which is unreal for his first month on the job, but he missed the smell of toner ink and coffee and fresh carpet glue, and the consistent 8-to-6 workday, and the predictable faceless geography of the suburbs. And this conversation was giving him a headache. They were going to seek out a goddess of Babylonia or Sumeria or Who-knows-where-ia. His Timex read 11:00. He had been awake for eighteen hours. He sighed. *My kingdom for a tumbler of rum, and a clean bed*, he thought.

Matta pecked him on the forehead, imparting an imprint of her glossy red lips. "Come on, Archie, loosen up." She tugged the triangular end of his blue rep tie, popping the knot, and then pried the overhand loop so that the ends rakishly drooped from his stiff collar.

"Woo hoo," he said flatly. "Where is the danger? Shall we sally toward it now?"

"That's c[ap]ital spirit, big A," warbled Guy, "Youngerman is *up* [to] something. I don't plan on [being] taken advantage of."

"What now, Guy" asked Lulu.

"Forthward! Let's [hop] through this curtain and [be]come literature!"

"What curtain?"

"*This* curtain." And there it was.

Chapter 5:
Man's Uproar

"Ouch."

"Damn it!"

"Who's d[ea]d?"

"I am!"

"Aleister, I swear [to] Almighty—"

"Where are we?"

"In the dark."

"I think I'm laying on s[o]mething sharp."

"That would be me."

"Ouch. What the hell [i]s *that*?"

"That would be the *other* me."

"This is just like that time in the Lamprey Room—"

"I told you to n[e]vereverneverev[e]r mention that again!"

Snick.

An intense shaft of illumination scraped through the darkness. Pinwheels of limbs. Sheens of gold. Glinty ricochets of a white beam of light.

Snick!

Snick

Snick!

Snick!

Snick.

Snick!

"OoooooooO," harmonized the Postmodernaires, a metallic echo formulating in the air.

More shafts of light crisscrossed the blackness, in strips of anatomical confusion and highlights of glaring brilliance. With silent delicacy, patent pump slipped from juxtaposed armpit, sleek leg uncurved from palpitating neck, and fine fingertips slunk from out of glossy lips.

As they stood up, and swayed their flashlights, they saw that this large chamber shone *completely* of gold. The imbricating geometries floating up the thick, fat columns were golden. The arches of the ceiling, an architecture of diminishing upside down Vs, were golden. And thirty feet above them, between two of those gilded arches, a threshold, tickled by the wisp of a damask curtain, was golden.

"I wonder whatever broke our fall," asked Archibald.

"Each oth[e]r," said Guy.

"That hardly seems—" muttered Archibald, before losing his train of thought. "Let's see now," he said, unfolding their contract once more, but by then every flashlight was exploring the twenty-four-caratscape. The vaulted space grooved inward like the brassy ribs of a whale in a visceral, heavenly procession, the passage through those glistering ogees bending, turning, whorling, until, over the sound of their footfalls, they heard the muffled sound of—a—human—voice.

Pace by pace, the arches dwindled down as the ceiling receded to an indigo door.

The human intonations were louder than before.

Guy nudged. The indigo door skewed inward.

Black-and-white checkered tiles flowed into a cupola of sandy rock. Their heels clicked forward, and they saw the shape of a woman slouching on a divan. The woman wore a gray Brooks pantsuit (circa 1975). The jacket was unfastened, one flap melting over the side of the red velvet cushioning, the other scantily covering the nakedness of her breast. Her knee bent up into the air, and her very tan bare foot was set atop the fuzzy red fabric, the toenails a glossy black. Her dark hair flowed into long pleats, which ended in little red tassels that seemed almost alive, like the tips of anemones.

Over her shoulder, everyone saw a floor console Magnavox, with the Brylcreemed perfection of a talking head gabbling in its bulbous screen, screens that reflected in miniature on the woman's aviator glasses.

"This is how it starts," she sighed.

"How *what* starts, exactly?" asked Lulu.

"One of those great eras of contestation between gods and man."

"And how do the men fare?" asked Archibald.

"Middling to rather badly. Actually, mostly badly."

"How badly?"

"Everyone dies."

"And what does middl[i]ng look like?" asked Guy.

"Nearly everyone dies."

"I see."

On the television, the man's face dissolved into a giant banana on a trapeze complaining about the need for a vacation. The aviators did not move, the woman's cheekbones imperturbable.

"Who are you?" asked Lulu.

"A votary, of course."

"A priestess—of Ishtar?"

"I hope you are not the *smart* one in this group."

"Hmmmm," said Lulu. "Where is she?"

"My lady? She's around here somewhere. She's expecting you. You are early, however."

"Early for what?"

Beneath the mirrored shades, a smirk crept up those tawny cheekbones.

"Oh come on, old girl, tell us," said Aleister, flouncing

upon the edge of the divan.

The smirk became a little sneer, but Ishtar's votary made no other gesture. After a shortish while, though, she spoke again.

"You are here to play your part."

"Pray tell, wh[a]t parts are those?"

"You'll see quite soon enough. I hope you *are* ready."

Everyone felt an awful squinching of inner ears, the television flickering.

"Whatever was that?" asked Aurora, her forearms pinching the sides of her feathery red hair.

"Many of the gods are starting to, err, grumble."

"Why?"

"Because you are making too much noise. Their slumbers are crimped, and if they cannot sleep, then they cannot—there are consequences."

"*We* are making too much noise?"

"Not you in particular, not that *that* shall be any great distinction when—"

"What did you mean," interrupted Lorrie, "when you said *consequences*."

"There'll be wrath, of course."

"Catastrophic wrath?" asked Aurora, smoothing the slender pleats of her Murakami poodle skirt.

"Is there any other sort?" asked the votary of Ishtar.

"Heavens ripped asunder, like in a global flood?" asked Lulu, holding the cuneiform journal against her chest.

"Drip drop drip."

"How often has this happened before?" asked Lorrie.

"Five or so times, but none for epochs and epochs."

"The Tower of Babel fell that way?" challenged Lulu.

"The first time," mused the votary.

"For the very vain vanity of elevating their language closer to the divine?" asked Lulu.

"It was babbling before it was ten stories up."

"And why is there too much noise now?" asked Aurora.

The woman focused her gaze upon the Magnavox.

More near-paralytic squinching, and the television flared its white noise and ash.

"Communication satell[i]tes," guessed Guy, his head sidelong, a huge finger lodged deep into the ampersand whorl of his ear. "They chuck our bad noise *way* upstairs, [don't] they?"

The votary smirked.

"Hold on," said Aleister, "are you saying that our various sputniks are scraping the underside of Heaven?"

"It's not the amount of interstellar doodads, mind you," she said, "it's just how much rubbish they all have to say for themselves, and how loudly they say it."

"This is nonsense," huffed Lorrie with a judo swoop to the air. "Space is relative. There is no heaven, no *literal* heaven, at any rate, for there is no astronomical palace in the air, none that very good telescopes can see, anyway, and we are on a round planet, so there could be no circumference round enough for there to be an up there the world round. Not even the universe, or multi-verse, round."

The votary pursed her lips, with little Ray Harryhausen scorpions reflected over her eyes. "The gods are always above all things, wherever you are."

"Then why is Ishtar, ummmmm, *down* here?" asked Lulu softly.

"Negotiating, silly."

"With whom?" asked Simone.

"Mr. Youngerman," said Archibald.

"No," said the votary, "although he is involved, I daresay. My lady is rather miffed with him, though."

"Whatever for?"

"He decorated the room outside. She didn't like it."

"A bit ostentatious," said Lulu, "I can see that—and,

like, *any* sort of stairway would have been nice."

"And th[e]re's *no* bar," suggested Guy.

"Why are we talking about this?" Lulu asked the votary, "How long have you been here?"

"In this temple or in this cavern?"

"You were here *before* this ziggurat was moved?"

"Oh yes."

"In the late nineteenth century?"

"I suppose."

"My head is starting to hurt," said Lulu, swirling her fingers through her temples, mussing the straight fringe of her auburn bangs.

"There, th[e]re," cooed Guy, kissing her forehead with his black glossy lips. "So," he said to the votary, "Your lady needs our ass[i]stance?"

"I don't suppose you have seen anything like—a—stone tablet laying around?"

"No," sang the Postmodernaires.

And then Lorrie added, "There are apparently alternate versions of the twelve tablets of *Gilgamesh* here. Which is the one you want?"

"The thirteenth."

"But *Gilgamesh* has only twelve tablets!" sniped Lulu.

"So: haven't seen it?"

"Sigh."

"Didn't think so. Still: keep a keen eye."

"Sure thing."

"So where *is* Ishtar?" asked Archibald.

"You had better go find her," said the votary, pointing at another indigo door across the cupola. "Now please shoo. My show is coming on."

Chapter 6:
The Terrors of Ignorance

"I don't see how that other door could have *even* led anywhere since we walked in a spiral to get to that room," muttered Lulu as they streamed into another corridor illuminated by kerosene torches. "It's as if the structure is mutating. Are we somehow walking *up*?"

"This *is* the zig-zaggiest ziggurat I've ever seen," said Blee.

"Everybody stick cl[o-se]," growled Guy, strutting past millennia-old *bas-reliefs*, shadows leaping up.

"Wait," said Archibald, "shouldn't we try to get our bearings before we—"

"No," said Guy, "better to get them *while* pressing on."

"How do we do that?" sputtered Archibald.

"Lulu," said Guy, tugging both Blee and Archibald forward by their shirt-cuffs as he stumped by, "what['s] going on in this pyramid?"

"I don't—"

"Don't, and I mean *do not*, say—"

"But—"

"Do try to guess, darling."

"Something that woman back there said."

"It was rude," bleated Blee, pinching his purple soul-patch, "her not inviting us to watch TV with her."

"Silence, you. We *are* the show. Lulu, *wh*[a]*t* did the wom[an] say?"

"That the gods can no longer sleep."

"Meaning?"

"I don't quite know. It's a metaphysical puzzle, a poly-theological quandary well outside my own customary areas of inquiry."

"Do try to keep guessing, darling."

"All right-o, Crito: what if this ziggurat isn't the *only* thing that's changing?"

"What if."

"Well, these dozing deities are so thoughtlessly hassled, become perturbed spirits, and—then—the structure of all the stories might be changing as well."

"You're saying, the stories [o]f Gilgamesh. The stories of Ishtar."

"At the very least. You see, it is as if these narratives are enjoined by a living fabric of consciousness, and are not just words on a page—or etchings on a tablet."

"As if the stories are in the consciousness of the gods, you're saying."

"As if the stories *are* the consciousness of the gods."

"Why do you think so?"

"The merest intuitional hunch, *jefe*. I mean, perhaps Mr. Youngerman is delusional, and that votary scant more than a couch tart who's fled a rubber cell somewhere, and maybe Mr. Y spiked our champagne at dinner, and maybe these architectural anomalies are the wafting discords of our poisoned serotonin levels—but even this very long nexus of iffy ifs doesn't explain us sharing the *same* hallucinations."

"This *is* a touch m[ore] strange than normal, [is]n't it?"

"Several touches, I would say."

"Yeah. You have a point, I suppose, but [I] still don't grasp h[ow] the epic is now reweaving its[e]lf, in the woofy warp [o]f divine mind. What does that [e]ven mean? More plainly, please."

"*Gilgamesh* is *trying* to reweave itself, despite the interference, the dissonance of—"

"—All th[ose] chatter-spewing satellites. You haven't answ[ered] my question."

"I suppose we'll find out. This is quite serious."

"Yes," said Guy philosophically.

"I see," he added, more philosophically.

"Who c[a]res?" he finally droned.

"We do," said Lulu.

"Why?"

"Because we're *in* the story."

"I don't und[e]rstand."

"I don't either, to tell you the truth."

"How can *we* be [in] a story?"

"How can we be outdoors right now?"

"What [are] you talking about?"

"Look up."

Guy halted. Atop them, luminescent pinpricks tinkled in the inky void. Guy cackled a little cackle. The Man waved his overlarge mitts in the musty air over his head, poking at the nothing, which is to say, *failing* to poke at the nothing.

"There is no ceiling anymore, chief. That's pure sky."

"Where are w[e]?"

"Mesopotamia, perhaps. But the trickier question is *when* are we."

"Why? What t[i]me does the bar close?"

"It's already closed, *mon chat fou.*"

Frenetic spires of electrified hair whizzed forward. "Come, come," said Lorrie, "tell us *when* we are—or, umm, *were?*"

Lulu tilted her head, an auburn bang unfurling over a glistening cheekbone, her eyes abstracting nightward, the leatherbound journal curled in her arms against her chest.

"Sweetie, Rodin is rusting. Spill it."

"We aaaaaaaare," said Lulu, biting her glossy china-glaze lips, "somewheres betweeeeen the seventh and thirteenth centuries?"

"I see."

"Not yet, you don't. The story, if reaching aback to the *real* story, might date to an actual—historical—Gilgamesh, circa the twenty-eighth century, B. C. E., give or take a fortnight."

"So you're saying you don't know?" sniped Lorrie.

"Umm, sure."

"So what's next?" asked Archibald. "We can't spend Mr. Youngerman's money if we don't get out of here."

"And we need to [get the] hell to the Sabre Room," added Guy. "Forthward?"

"Yeah," said Lulu, "let's do that."

The passage extended before them in a procession of firelight, leading them this way and that, the torch flames sometimes bending into the darkness, and as they walked the Postmodernaires made the occasional synchronized pirouette, unable to repress themselves even in this subterranean lair, until the walls of the corridor lowered closer to the ground, until the corridor itself terminated in a shallow dead-end three feet tall, and was marked by an inscription on white stone:

CONSIDERING WHAT MEASURES MAY BE BEST
FOR THE SANCTITY OF PUBLIC COMFORT,
CONSUMPTION OF WINE
OR ALCOHOL IN ANY OF ITS VARIOUS FORMS
IN THIS REALM IS HEREBY FORBIDDEN BY SACRED
DECREE OF KING GILGAMESH. DIRECTIVE MLVIII.

THIS MEANS YOU, MR. PSYCHO.

NOT A DROPLET.

Guy squinted his left eye shut, gazing at the etchings, and then the air resounded with the horrific decibels of a fantod roaring itself from the very cells of his diaphragm through the molecules all around them. Out, and out, and out, this electrified yawp of despair. Guy kicked his glossy wingtips through the dirt, leaving a wake of dust, himself nearly tripled-over, his fingers frizzing his short, graying hair. The entirety of the entourage stared at him as he then vilified those clod-stomping Paleolithic nabobs who were our ancestors, down to their very electrons doing unsavory things to all those decaying neutrons, and the protons whose sexual experiences may have included their own grandmothers. The actual sanity of all quarks everywhere past and present was then called into question. And then the Man thrashed the bas reliefs with his enormous fists, leaving deep, knuckle-shaped indentations in the soft stone, brownish dust puffing out from every crackling punch, fragments of ancient sculpture littering their feet. The Postmodernaires tittered, even Lulu, while Archibald looked on, gray ellipses beneath his eyes, and the band was impassive, except for Aleister, who watched this outburst so tensely that the scar down his neck squirmed.

And then Guy stopped. "I don't like th[i]s Gilgamesh character."

"I can see that," said Trudy.

"So what do we do now?" asked Archibald. "There is no more forthward."

"[U]p is the new forthward!" With two large strides, Guy ascended the sandy mess that was once the little wall at the corridor's end, and then dusted himself off. With some bustling, the rest of his crew likewise ascended into the night. The party spread out over the area. Looking down at the groove below that was the corridor,. There were certain patterns that it made, that Lulu saw. She pulled out the leather-bound journal and squinted.

"What?" asked Archibald.

"The tunnel we were in—it's in the shape of cuneiform."

"That's weird," said Archibald.

"I think we've found the fifth tablet," said Lulu.

"M-hm?" said Guy.

"We're standing on it."

Chapter 7:
Humbaba's Splendors

"Hmmm," said Trudy, staring down into the shadowy chasms below them. She contorted her cherry red smile as if trying to recreate the impossible wanderings of stone that had brought them to this present spot, and she went on to wonder how strange it was that those impossible wanderings were also somehow the impossible wanderings of her mind, or her mind trying to follow the ancient words or symbols or etchings of someone or something else's mind. And then she wondered how they could have wandered down that tunnel at all, since this cuneiform carved into the earth was not even a continuous line, which meant that—but as she turned her head to the stream of unintelligible signifiers behind her, *there* was the ziggurat, menacing the dark open air, without Mr. Youngerman's cavern. "We aren't underground anymore," she said on her tip-toes.

"We're not anywhere, really," said Lulu.

And then: "Look," said Lulu, pointing with two fingers, her nails vermillion, across the expanse of elongated cuneiform. In the middle distance, the brown earth gave way to a blue mist, which then gave way unto a green expanse of distant trees. The entourage scuffled through the margins of the inscribed earth towards the strange wood, heels tentative on the soft ground.

"Either we're in Appalachia right now," Lulu said, "or else we're in the Forbidden Forest."

"Or bo[th]?" added Guy.

"If there is a Forbidden Forest, why are we headed near it?" asked Archibald, with his pale fingers tracing through his brown, curly hair. "It's ummm, still forbidden, right?"

"We need to keep going," said Lulu. "We need to get to the *heart* of the forest."

"Hold on: shouldn't we discuss whether to go back?" said Archibald. "We have a gig."

The entourage turned to look back, at the matrix of characters leading back to the ziggurat and the empty, black sky.

"Sh[a]ll we take a vote?" asked Guy.

"Fine, I get it," Archibald said. "Let's go. Let's go."

They stepped into the wispy arabesques of blue haze, cool, tingly, and sentient, and through the deteriorating fog they passed into brilliant green monotonies of cedars, down and up and up and down the resiny swells of earth, not encountering a single creature, not a squirrel or an owl or even a speck of an ant, while every tree was a masterpiece of sculpture, trees stood like souls, spires rising greenly into a bright, black sky. The bluish mist hovered motionless at their feet, as if time itself were still.

"Even in the time of Gilgamesh's reign," taught Lulu, "ancient Mesopotamia was not a fertile place."

"Is this the historical Gilgamesh, or the mytho-literary one?" asked Matta.

"Pay attention, please. We're talking subsistence farming, for the most part, and there were few trees available for lumber, for building things."

"I.e., they happened to be resource-poor," added Archibald, trying to keep his glistering tasseled loafers un-smudged.

"Quite," said Lulu. "So while some accounts—including some versions of the epic—have Gilgamesh almost inexplicably setting out to face the keeper of the Forbidden Forest for some über-masculine glory-ride, there is reason to believe that he was actually on a quest deep outside his own country to gather the materials his world needed to thrive."

"Like Prometheus, but with wood instead of fire?" suggested Aurora, her red hair itself suggestive of flame.

"Is this a good idea?" asked Archibald, to which Trudy shrugged.

"Um," said Trudy, resting her hand upon his shoulder. "You're doing fine."

"Am I?"

"Did you expect all this, when you signed on?"

"Honestly, no. I mean, I knew he was—you know—but is *this* normal?"

"This is a *little* abnormal, I suppose."

"Does this ever bother you—working for him?"

"It's the greatest party I've ever been too. When we're dark, I do tend to go comatose, though."

"Do you trust *him*?"

"With my life. We all do. We always have."

"And how long is always?"

"Going on three years."

"Until the end of time?"

"Until the end of the party. Are you going to stick with us?"

"Should I?"

"Most definitely."

"Why?"

"Two reasons. One, I like you."

Archibald rubbed his chin, to conceal the blush spreading across his face. "And two?"

"He needs you. He really needs you."

"I'll tell you what he needs."

"Don't," Trudy said.

After an uncomfortable minute, Arch asked, "Does he really need that much protection?"

"Only when approached from north-northwest."

"I'm sorry," he said.

"But yes. Don't disrespect the party."

"I truly am sorry," said Archibald, back-stepping in front of her.

"Do you really not like him?" Trudy asked.

"I don't know," he said, "I never thought I would score the interview."

"Why did you apply?"

"I don't know if I like *him*, but I love his music. Is it stupid, to want to work for someone because you love his music?"

Trudy put her arm in his. "No, not at all."

"Goody."

"Is it possible that we are just walking around in circles here?" asked Lorrie.

"Euh meh, I mus stohp for *une* momen," mumbled Philippe. He removed a pack of American Spirits from his black watch plaid trousers and slipped a cigarette between his pale, thin lips as he slouched against a tree trunk. No one looked in his direction as he ignited the Spirit and sucked deeply, the tip burning red, then black.

Philippe's mouth and the cylinder produced a gray plume into the air as Guy, gazing into the perplexing perspective of the tree lines, the vertical world of cedars, breathed in the mountain air, the Gaultier gauze encircling his neck tightening. "It all looks the [sa]me," said Guy, rubbing his big oval jaw. "How will we know when we [ha]ve found the heart of the forest?"

An acute squinching made everyone clutch their ears, and a seismic thump vibrated their marrow and quivered the needles on the cedars around them.

And then a *thump* of even greater magnitude boomed.

The very trunks of those majestic trees now winced with each savage smiting of the earth. Archibald did his best to reach up into a tree, looking like a piñata on a blustery day. Simone dug the spike heels of her patent pumps into the dry grass of the ground. Guy stood still, his legs apart, the little front flip of his gray-dark hair shuddering.

The ground wobbled as a great yellow beast emerged from the trees. He loomed fifteen feet tall with an anatomy much thicker than a man's, but worst of all, was the face, if it even could be called a face—its features, its countenance, was (or seemed to be) nothing more or less than an eminence of entrails.

"Thou hast found the *navel* of the forest," wheezed the monster in a mucusy voice.

"Will the navel d[o]?" Guy asked Lulu.

Lulu shrugged.

"Hey," Guy said to the monster, "You speak English."

"Nope."

"No?"

"We converse in the language of the dream-tongue."

"Um, all right. Shouldn't y[ou] put some pants on? There are rosebuds present."

"It is *my* forest," sniffed the giant.

"He has a point," Guy granted.

"He doesn't even have parts," said Archibald.

"Yes, but it *is* st[i]ll distracting," said Guy.

"Great Humbaba," said Lulu, genuflecting, her auburn bangs scraping down her glittery cheekbones, "we come by Ishtar's bidding, and wish no harm or insult to this sacred place."

"That is the ugliest park ranger I've ever seen," said Aleister, nudging Blee in the ribs.

"Sh!" said Lulu.

"O dear Maker," added Blee, "dig the halitosis on him."

"You're just noticing that now?" asked Simone.

There appeared in the front of Humbaba's head an arching of a bowelly equivalent of eyebrows, as if deciding upon an emotion, or maybe just thinking, or digesting, a thought.

"Great Humbaba—" said Lulu.

"Ask about the thirteenth tablet," interrupted Guy.

"Working on it," huffed Lulu.

"Depart at once. Touch not a *single* part of the forest."

"Do we look like lumberjacks to you?" asked Aleister. "What could we even hurt this forest with?"

Philippe emitted a feline, sangfroidy sigh as he exhaled two parallel lines of smoke from his nostrils, noticing how the grey lines flowed into the mist, which became less of a scrim now, how the shades of misty gray congealed in a Kandinskyesque outline of nothing in particular, how the fog amounted to a symbol of, well, of itself, a penumbral abstraction that was almost as delicious as the smoke, a mesmeric observation to have as he released the ember-ended butt of his cigarette onto the grass floor of the forest.

"Oh poo," said Lulu.

"Hey!" said Guy as Humbaba hefted him by his chalk-striped lapels, the gurgly grousing of the monster swooping across the forest. Guy shoved a size fourteen wingtip onto the beast's chest and accidentally backflipped, landing fleetly afoot, much to his own surprise. Instantaneously, generations of evolutionary instincts flung him into a rope-a-dope fit of pugilistic bouncitude. Humbaba charged back towards him, in an absolute quaking that unbalanced everyone.

"H[o]ld on, hold on!" yelled Guy, clutching a cedar.

The great creature's facial markings wiggled inscrutably, its body pausing.

Guy doffed his jacket, and then tossed it to Simone. His midnight blue shirt looked crisp underneath his black braces. After rolling up his cuffs, Guy projected his underhanded thick fists at the foul titan, and upraised his chin.

"If only Wog and Wonk were here," said Simone.

"Ind[ee]d," said Guy. "This is their sort of thing."

Humbaba's fleshy hand clenched over Guy's head, and the Man's body lifted off the ground and swung in a circle over Humbaba like a sloppy lariat. Guy pounded his fists against the giant's grip, a gadfly's sting, and his kicks did not even land upon the creature's flesh—just these spastic, chalk-striped gyrations of legs.

Matta marveled at how sparkling even the soles of Guy's shoes looked in the misty dark.

"Juke and move!" said Aleister.

"Where the *@&$* is [Gilg]amesh!" screamed Guy in a Doppler warping of noise, his toe-tips scraping the trees. His arms flailed, trying to find something to cling to, and what his fingers alit upon was something unthinkably like an anthropomorphic sausage, turgid but throbbing alive in liquid madness.

The roar was an elephantine mélange of amphibian howl, whale-like soughing, and blistering white noise that transformed in the dream-tongue language as a deafening, "NOT THE FACE! NOT THE FACE!"

Guy was hurled aground.

The monster clutched at the front of its fearful head, wailing, injured beyond even the comprehension of the gods.

"Hey," said Guy, as he clambered to his feet, "Calm down, big f[e]lla. Didn't m[ean] it."

"What is wrong with you?" the giant said, stepping

backwards, timbering colossal trees in its panic. Wrinkles of flesh wept crystalline ichor as the fleshly mass of thing writhed. The air seemed contaminated with both a coppery tang and carbonic ash.

"Humbab[a]?" asked Guy, "sir?"

There was a crack, cedars snapping in their middles, and the creature was reduced to two hands clutching ripped trunks. The entourage rushed forward to find a ravine swallowing the terrified giant, the tubular protrusions of its face gasping—and then the two cedars (uprooted in his hands) tumbled with him into the gorge. Humbaba shrank into nothing, nothing except an inaudible whirring.

"What the Hell just happened?" screamed Guy, yanking on his jacket.

Lulu looked pallid, bereft of speech.

Everyone stared down into the empty scar of the land, awaited some horrible report from the bottom of the abyss. Silence.

And then there was a ubiquitous frizzling behind them, around them, and when they turned to look, a surge of incandescent smoke unfurled over them as the yellow-orange madness of conflagration spat its way from bough to bough across the Forbidden Forest, a cordon of flame closing in on them.

"What do we do?" yelled Aurora.

"[Exit]!" said Guy. "Stage anywhere!"

They ran to the torn footing of the black crevasse, and fled left and right around its wide opening through sickening tufts of smoke. The blaze chased them as they tried to keep their footing.

As they reached the other side of the ravine, four hundred feet away, the forest on either side of them somehow assumed the form of lanes of trees. These lanes thickened into hedge-lined paths. The entourage had sundered itself into several scurrying parties.

By the time the blaze disappeared, what had seemed like threatening smoke was now the subtlest, gentlest blue mist once again. Like the whitest of white mice, Guy Psycho and his entourage found themselves within a maze.

Chapter 8:
In the Maze of Reddest Mind

Trudy pounded on the hedge with her balled fists, her black ringlets quivering, and yet when she turned around to Mr. Fitzpatrick her face was consumed by her big, cheeky smile. "This, then," she said, touching her cherry-red upper lip with the tip of her tongue, "won't be the way out."

"No," sighed Archibald.

Trudy paced the turf between the foliage walls, her anklebones wobbling. The silver ruffles of her party dress looked hypnotic. Archibald gazed down, and was disappointed by his smudged loafers, even though he was still surprised to be alive.

"Say, clasp your hands in front of you, please," said Trudy.

"Why?" asked Archibald, but by then her heavy sole was atop his interlaced fingers and her stomach pressed against his crushed nose. "Oh," he said. "Can you see anything?"

"Mm-hmm," she said, and then there was a—snap—and then she eased down from his hands with the silky red bloom of a damask rose, which, with some deliberation, she affixed behind her left ear, just poking out of her black curls. "That's better. Don't you agree?"

"Don't you think we should—why, yes, it does, actually."

"Thank you."

"So what do we do now?"

"We have a look around, of course."

"You're not afraid?"

"Of a hedge?"

"Of being ensnared in a nefarious plot that is spiraling out of control?"

"No, not very," said Trudy, "Not *yet*, anyway. Shall we?"

And thus Trudy and Archibald hurried deeper into the horticultural confusion, the faint, indirect glow of dusk blurring their way.

Quite elsewhere, the grass was twitching in the dusking light, the moon a premature ghost low in the sky. The air was tinged with carbon and Chanel number 12. Matta stood on the pointy tiptoes of her silver go-go boots, the just-singed frills of her diaphanous dress swooshing with the mist. "Marco!" she yelled to the empty maze.

"Polo," sang Guy.

"Polo" called Aurora.

(("Polo" called Aleister.))

Matta stood erect, her vampiric canines poised in the air. "Olly olly oxen free!" she yelled.

"Ouch!" said Aleister.

"Tut," said Guy.

"Gnash," said the hedgerow.

"Come on!" said Matta.

"We're doing it," said Aurora, "keep your bra on." And she turned the corner and came into view, in a poodle skirt depicting an apocalyptic Murakami cartoon face, and Mary Janes. Her red hair, feathering out from her ruddy cheekbones, made her look like she was flying.

Aleister limped out on the *other* extremity of the grassy aisle.

"The fire's gone?" asked Aurora, rubbing her ankles.

"I think so," said Aleister. "Didn't I hear the Man just now?"

"Boss?" Matta said.

"Oomph," said Guy, bursting through the green wall, *not* mussing his suit, despite the near quantum impossibility of that happening.

"How did you do that?"

"I think gr[een] thoughts, imagine [the] taste of [whi]skey, and let [nat]ure take its course."

"You attune yourself to the powers of intention?" asked Matta.

"Can you [not] feel it?"

"Do you know what you are talking about?"

"Haven't the sl[i]ghtest," said Guy.

"Do it again," Aurora suggested. "That trick could be our ticket out of here."

"D-okay!" said Guy, bounding through the hedge once more.

"*Trés* good," said Matta, "now come back."

The hedge did not even twitch.

"Boss?' asked Matta, her eyebrow arching, a taut smile peeling over her white, pointy teeth. "I guess I should have seen that coming," she mused.

Vernita *rushed* to a green dead-end, about-

faced, and rushed back down the pathway, turning left rather than right.

The yellow satin of her miniskirt swished with each of her strides. Her size seven ballet flats felt buoyant on the turf. The black polo's upraised collar grazed the bottom rim of her medium-sized afro.

There were, she thought, slowing down, three ways to beat a maze.

First, the maze-walker could *try* to memorize, in something like a photographic fashion, *all* of the paths she has chosen, thus through trial-and-error ruling out the wrong ways until the *right* way is happened upon. This was, she thought, a futile strategy.

Second, the maze-walker could try *not* to memorize all of the paths she has chosen, and walk willy-nilly for as long as her feet would carry her, in the inevitability that she would happen to *accidentally* happen upon the right way. This was, she thought, another futile strategy for a maze this flipping humongous.

Third, the maze-walker could try not to think of *anything* at all, and let her feet work somehow as unconscious extensions of her mind, and so according to the Taoist principle of *p'u*, beat the maze by accepting the maze absolutely as a maze, without fighting its maze-ness as a maze, or vying for dominance at all. Just *being*, and letting the maze *be*. This was, she thought, another futile strategy, but if one embodies the spirit of *p'u*, then it wouldn't feel like a futile strategy, would it? But in that case a strategy isn't even a strategy at all, and escaping the maze, even if one succeeded, wouldn't matter at all. She needed to hurry.

Vernita came to another green dead-end, about-faced, and walked down the pathway, turning left rather than right.

Every blade of grass she trod upon was felt in the soles of her feet.

Then Vernita heard a murmuring. Voices, the basso reverberations through the walls of foliage, were perhaps nearby.

"Hey!" she called.

"Mmmbbbumumum," said the other side of the hedge.

"Can you hear me?"

"Blablumbloomoom," said the other side of the hedge.

Vernita waited a moment, to see if the murmuring responded to her. But she didn't hear anything anymore. She marched forthward.

Guy Psycho burst from one green wall and managed a wave before his momentum carried him through the next wall. She ran forward, and tried to probe the evergreen plane with her finger.

"Chief?"

"Mfloblumind," said the hedge.

"Chief?"

Silence.

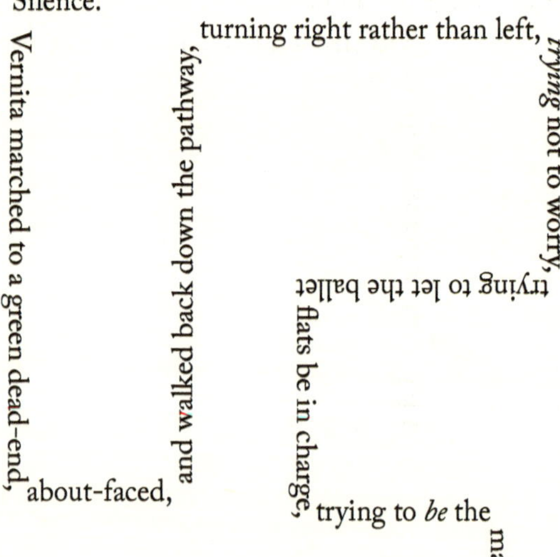

Somehow, Aurora had lost the others.** She thought she had heard something on the other side of the hedge, and stopped, watching Aleister rush straight down the row. "Wait," she whispered, but years of decibel abuse had left the guitarist hard of hearing. She crept a few feet forward, now feeling the ficus leaves tickle her bare legs.

"Hello?" she said to the hedge.

"Mampropololodoom!" responded the hedge.

Aurora sprinted forward on her pumps, her hands swaying at her sides to keep balance.

"Aleister!" she shouted.

She stopped at a wall, and turned left with the passage, and then right, to a fork in the path.

"Aleister?"

The blue mist seemed to be seeping in through the roots of the hedges. It felt cool on the tops of her feet, and up her calves. Upside down, the maniacal manga design grinned at her from her poodle skirt. It didn't seem cool anymore: a bona fide bad omen, that distorted mouse face, these curlicues of groping mist.

Aurora strutted left, trying to walk fast without conveying panic, even though she *seemed* to be the only person there. Such nervousness was unlike her. She attended four years of Juilliard, knowing Manhattan at *all* hours, including sobering crawls through Hell's Kitchen back to her fifth-floor walk-up, so. Which way did Aleister and the others go?

"Marco!" she yelled.

Nothing. Aurora looked up at the sky, which held no stars, although the dusk had been rapid, and the

---

**The publisher invites those readers who are made anxious by tight narrative spaces to make this a select-your-own-misadventure by jumping to page 78. For those who stay, courage!*

moon seemed low in the sky *somewhere*. Was this some cosmic practical joke? Was the sky the ceiling of a stage? Would Mr. Youngerman pop out and tell them to start the show?

"Guy, where are you?" she wondered. Nothing bothered her when she was with him. When he wasn't wearing sunglasses, his blue-green eyes, beneath the darkened kohl of his eyelids, seemed to *see* so much in the world, in whatever was happening. His mottled irises, which seemed to contain two galaxies each. She always avoided staring. She didn't want to give him the wrong idea. Or the right idea. She was scared for him.

"Hello?"

When the smoke no longer pricked her nostrils, Pasha's paces slowed from a sprint to a skip, her red Art Deco dress galloping in the air, the minute fluff of her black angora sweater feeling warm upon her skin and—*wham*! She collided into the wall of a rosebush and bounced aground, akimbo, and unladylike. Her black hair sprayed across her pale face and the dark lenses of her white Wayfarers.

Someone stepped behind her. "Oj!" screamed Pasha.

"It's me," said Lorrie, kneeling down and grabbing beneath Pasha's armpits. "Up you go," she said, hefting the chorus girl up.

"*Spasibo*, you," said Pasha.

"Mm-hmm."

"Where are we?"

"Somewhere between point A and point Z."

"Point Q?"

"My *best* guess is somewhere between D and H."

"Imagine that!"

"I am trying *not* to."

"Why is that, friend?"

"Hey."

"What?"

Lorrie traced her finger above the shadowy angle of Pasha's cheekbone, along a jagged line of blood. "This place is thorny," Lorrie said. "We need to be careful."

Pasha took her white Wayfarers off and stared at the leafy wall, which by some trick of the moonlight seemed to be smiling at her. "Damn," said Pasha." She extracted a small scarf from her sleeve and pressed its black silk to her wounded cheek. Then she gazed at Lorrie, the bristling barbs of the keyboardist's hair curving around the auricle of her ear, stopping at the sharp angle of her jaw. Her eyes were so large, glassy and black. Lorrie smiled, the laugh-lines around her mouth rippling, complicating her rouged cheekbones. Pasha smiled her pert little smile. She pushed her Wafarers back over her eyes.

The hedge rustled.

"Let's get out of here," said Pasha.

Blee zoomed between them and smashed into the hedge, wedging inside mid-stride, one tuxedo leg up, one tuxedo leg down, a decaying canvas sneaker protruding from the wall. "Mmrrouughhhnk!" he yelled. "Mmrrouuuughh mleeeee mlounnk! Mowwwffffth ffflunk mlaaaaaaaa!"

Pasha convulsed so much that she had to embrace Lorrie. Lorrie stood nearly impassive, her sparkling spikes casting little shadows on Pasha's face, but even Lorrie's mouth hinted a silvery smile at this $R_1U_1M_3P_3U_1S_1$ Blee was making—the frantic toe of one shoe expressing volumes of his panic.

Within ten seconds the two women heaved him out of the hedge's grasp. He flopped down, and stooped before them spitting and hacking out little leaves. "Thhhankthss," he eventually gasped with his bloodied tongue, globules of vermillion spouting onto his satiny lapels.

"Mm-hmm," said Lorrie.

And *thwack!* went Aurora into the hedge.

The blue wisps of mist chilled Tania, even though the air itself, in this rapid dusk, felt hot and dry against her calves and hands and face. No grasshoppers chirped, no cicadas droned. Above the green gaps of the hedges, the sky looked slate gray and freckled beige and brown.

She focused in front of her: these millions of small green zero-shapes suspended from shrubs, conforming to a geometric ideal that could never exist in nature. She pondered the enormity of the gardening this must entail.

The mist traced the back of her neck, slithering behind the tight filaments of her brunette ponytail. Sweat was beading on her upper lip, over the glossy pinkness of her lips. Tania shivered.

She embraced herself, and crossed one Mary Jane over the other, pressing her legs together for warmth. She felt the air breathe.

She patted down the silver sequins of her dress. She felt a tingling of coolness across her angular cheekbones, and over the slightly upturned tip of her nose. The dappled sky darkened between the greens.

"Flow with the go," she said, and took a tentative step forward on her Mary Janes. Her heels wobbled on the grassy footing. She reached out a steadying hand to the hedge wall while she walked.

The path turned to the right, and she followed it twenty feet down.

The path turned to the right, and she followed it twenty feet down, with slow, steady steps.

twenty feet down, with slow, steady steps.

The path turned to the right, and she followed it

The path turned to the right.

Tania pirouetted to gaze back down the corridor of the maze. She didn't *think* she had overlooked any other openings, which meant that she was either trapped in the maze or imagining that she was trapped in the maze, which meant that her mind was now, rather—

"What are you doing there?" asked Lulu.

"Waiting for you," whispered Tania.

Concetta's fingertips grazed the infinitudes of fig leaves on either side of the path, in this slick, waxy progression of sensation. Her kinked, dirty-blonde hair bounced with each step. Her long legs strode in intricate black floral hosiery, making her skin seem both irresistible and inhuman, like the design of some ethereal reptile's skin. The flouncing puffs of her mini-skirt scraped the garters that upheld the silk of her hose. Her tight-fitting blouse was unbuttoned at the bottom, from which her navel peeked between sculpted abs. Her thick-soled pumps made her sashaying, even with her arms outspread, an even-balanced affair, these strides through the peculiar blue fog hovering over the grass. She was smiling, which, with the naturally down-turned slant of her mouth, looked like a pouting smirk.

She was alive.

She was a Postmodernaire.

And, of course, she was Concetta.

"*Fah la me*," she trilled, "*Fah la do*."

Even more than the others, Concetta understood, at least on an intuitive level, what it meant to be both her fabulous self *and* a portion of that organism called the Postmodernaires. It was a family, or all the drops of wine that go into the bottle, and the cork, too. And she could drink the wine. She *loved* to drink the wine. Almost any wine. There would be more wine, and soon, she was certain. That Levantine woman or whoever she was would have some when they arrived at wherever they happened to be going. Or Guy would buy everyone a little something.

Her shoes knew the way. Concetta would *never* feel lost. But she needed to hurry.

Simone angled her bleeding foot up into the strip of fading light above. There wasn't much she could do about that little wound right now, but the offending pebble in her boot had been plucked out. She also felt a dull pain over her left eye socket. She guessed that she knocked skulls with *somebody* during their spastic exit from the fire. She lay flat on her back—with her long blond hair spread out on the turf—as she reached up, forced the knee-length boot back onto her calf, and laced the strings up her shin.

She positioned both her legs together in the air, and then leaned back on her bent arms, uplifting her lower back into the air as well. Then she let go, rolling her body, which (with a little shove of her shoulders) brought her to a standing position, the black satin tassels of her dress shimmying, with the sparkling lace of her petticoat puffing into place.

Her book, *Dioramas of the Inquisition*, was clutched in her hand. Simone whipped her hair to remove the dirt from the ground, but her hair seemed clean, as if the grass were artificial somehow. She scraped the immaculate grass with the pointed toe of her boot. It was, if anything was, real.

Right-i-o, thought Simone, *the thirteenth tablet, now.*

Simone was *assumed* to be the eldest of the Postmodernaires, although only Archibald knew her actual age, if her W-2 could be trusted. Simone had slight lines around her eyes, and she looked, somehow, too solid of demeanor to be in her mid-twenties. She might be thirty-two, or forty-two. Her hard green eyes defied curiosity. She matched the other Postmodernaires step-for-step, kick-for-kick, note-for-note.

Simone limped as the sky darkened above her.

"Oy!" she yelled.

For a millisecond, she saw Vernita's tall form—the yellow miniskirt glowing in the dark—strut across the path and disappear behind a shadowy green wall.

"V, stop!" yelled Simone, hastening. But the other Postmodernaire didn't return. When Simone arrived where Vernita had crossed, there wasn't even a cross-path. Simone stared with her hard green eyes at the wall. She blinked ahead to see if she miscalculated, but no new path seemed to open for a long way ahead.

"So *that's* how it's going to be."

She heard the tread of shoes. She squirmed around, with more agitation of black tassels, only to see Tania walking into a passage to her left.

"Hey!" said Simone, stalking towards the gap. She turned into the opening, which extended a long way, empty.

Up ahead, she heard something like Daphne's voice murmuring low.

"Helloo," Daphne called out.

No one replied.

Daphne charged forward.

"Can't you hear me?" she asked.

The woman in front of her, walking at Daphne's slowing pace, looked familiar: she stood 5'9" in her ankle boots. Her pleated, polka dot skirt swished with each lanky stride. Each arm swung alternately back and forth, the sleeve of the white shirt buttoned into a cuff just above the elbow. The wide lapels of the shirt, and the low cut, accentuated her pale chest, neck, and ethereal face.

As Daphne brushed a chestnut-brown lock of hair from her prominent forehead, so did the woman who was now only three feet in front of her.

"Narcissus, are you in there?" she asked her reflection.

"No, I didn't think so," answered Daphne and her doppelganger.

Daphne stepped forward, and knocked her knuckles against the mirror's surface. A slight tap rather than a deep, solid sound.

"Are you a clue, or a trap?" she asked herself.

She heard a knock from the mirror. Neither she nor her reflection had produced the noise.

Daphne leaped up in place, but the mirror was just too high, at least ten feet, to see over.

"Shave and a hair-cut," Daphne knocked.

Tap-tap, went the other side of the mirror.

"Can't you hear me at all?" asked Daphne.

No one replied.

Daphne scrutinized her image, which adhered to the fundamental laws of ocular physics: a Daphne with chestnut hair pouring behind her ears, curling around her pale neck. She stared with brilliant blue eyes at her very own brilliant blue eyes.

It was her high school years all over again.

And then: she remembered the fire, the tablet, and her sweet bandmates.

"You leave me no choice," Daphne said to the mirror.

She kicked her reflection, which shattered into the air, and onto the grassy ground.

"That is *sette anni* bad luck," said Concetta from the other side.

"Starting *when*?" asked Daphne.

Four hundred thirty-seven right angles away, Lulu and Tania had managed to find Alexis, Simone, and Philippe.

Lulu formulated a plan.

"You want me to do what?" snarled Tania.

"Look," said Lulu, "I'm not saying it *has* to be you. It could be Simone—"

"It couldn't," interrupted Simone.

"—or even myself. The point is we need to be able to find our way out, and since we have no rope or string, one of us *must* unravel her threads."

"You say that as if death were somehow not preferable to ruining this dress," fretted Tania. "This *couture* is not a sweater."

"We'll get you another."

"There is no other like this."

"O, come on."

"Hold on: you said it could be *you*?"

"Don't poke. I suppose it could be me." Lulu sighed, focused her-by-now tiny black pupils onto the hem of her dress and tried to pinch a thread out of the modular swirls of satin, but the fabric was too fine, too sartorially perfect, to yield.

"Here, let me help," huffed Simone, kneeling down, clutching the lace hem in both fists, and yanking.

"Why don't we just bleed ourselves and leave a trail of blood, or try disembowelment?" asked Tania.

"Where are your manners?" stammered Alexis.

"It's such a nice dress," cooed Tania. "There *has* to be another way."

"I hope so," murmured Simone, "this isn't ripping."

"Might these help?" said Philippe, holding out the coiled cords of bass strings.

"They might," said Lulu, taking them from his hand in the very moment that Simone rent one pleat of swirls from another on the dress, exposing Lulu's thigh.

"Ip!" said Tiana.

Lulu cupped her forehead in her hands. "We needed a thread, dear. This," indicating the slit in the silk, "is not quite a thread."

"In literature, this would be so much easier," said Simone.

"Indeed," said Lulu, strutting down the aisle, her dress spilling around her knee as she walked. Sighing, she squatted, the dress pooling around her high-heeled motorcycle boots, her black leather jacket collecting around her dress, and her auburn hair cascading around the collar of her black leather jacket. She squinted at the blurriness of the foursome clustered at the other end of the strip of maze, and her eyes burned with the exertion, the mist reasserting itself. She needed to concentrate. She needed to hurry.

Such a bad business, she thought. I am no match for this: I abandoned archeology, and these show business people still don't know what they are up against, or even know that they don't know what they are quite up against. They are, indeed, a liability. What would father do? What *did* father do when the team was inexperienced, or, jeez, when the land itself went mad against the inscrutabilities of time? Or did it never do that to him?

Her father was a ghost to her, even when she was young and he was alive, little more than a breath at the end of the dinner table, in those passages of time not consumed by some dig or another, while she fell in love with the Lerner and Lowe songbook, or Gregorian chant, or Postmodern dance, not to mention philosophy. Her father was of no use to her imagination, offered no escape or strategy for understanding this discovery she was experiencing, for she could not dream *his* next hypothetical move, or imagine what paper he might produce about this ziggurat (and what it is not), or what his intuition might have to tell about the debts of Fate.

"Are you going to pee, or what?" yelled Simone.

"Or what," muttered Lulu. She gazed up at the green surrounding them. "Philippe, lend me a boost, please?"

"You already have a nice one, *mon chéri.*"

"A *boost*, Philippe, a *boost*—lift me up?"

"Ahhh, *tout le suite.*"

Lulu diggled up into his grasp, and (a blush suffusing her glistening cheeks) looked up over the tip of the hedge. It was difficult to make anything out at first— just fog and dark sky—but if she leaned back (hold on Philippe) she saw rising up, that is, well—ahoy— something unbelievable.

"What is it?" asked Tania, with a flick of her silky, brunette ponytail.

"I *think* it's Mr. Youngerman," she said. Up high on the face of the mountain, a balcony protruded. From its height, a slender form gazed down with oversized eyes. Beside this miniature Mr. Youngerman, his wife, Trish, leaned with her arms upon the railing, her pink cocktail dress shimmering, a pink pump swinging through the gaps in the balustrade. The very red, pointed beard of Reginald stood somewhere behind them. Lulu waved. Their patron lowered his binoculars, and waved back.

"Are you sure that's Mr. Y?" asked Tania.

"I wish I wasn't."

"So what do we do now?" asked Simone.

"Okay," said Lulu, reaching inside her leather jacket, "I have an idea."

Guy unbuttoned his jacket as he sauntered through the wispy milky nothing of the air and felt the weariness of his legs, like leaking marrow, rather than the muscular gravity he *ought* to be feeling with drink. The loamy ground seemed to spring upon his toes, though. Was that a blue ghost of a man in a khaki suit? "All your innocence, and your bl[a]ndishments," he sang for no particular reason, other than to hear his own voice. "*Think*, you s[il]ly mimbo, think!"

As he walked, the ficus leaves evolved into skeletons, a dense complexus of sinister bone. He dropped a mint onto the ground, where it disappeared in the dirt with a sickening slurp. Guy placed the *next* mint into his mouth. Exhaled. He pressed his finger to a femur in the hedge, which did not budge. The black sockets of a skull stared him down. He moved forward down the pathway, which no longer opened up into its labyrinthine options, but rose up as if onto a hill, while the walls themselves engorged and transformed as he walked, the bones compacting into stone, and the stone coloring into silver and brassy deposits, which became enveined with circuits, wires and tubes and valves, which smoothened into a frosted layer of blueish glass. And then it wasn't only blue: there was a gigantic face, replicated and replicated and replicated in those replications, gazing at Guy from both sides of the maze, and now below himself too: but the face that gazed upon him was his own, back lips downturned. "All your inn[o]cence, and your blandishments," said the Guys in the televisions, "Were all [you] had t[o] impart."

"*You*," warbled Guy, "are the annihilator [of] my heart."

"Not a big hit for you," said the replications, their voices overlapping.

"Not in volume, but the [ditty] has its fans," Guy answered.

"We happen to know one of them."

"Since you are me, you [sho]uld know plenty of them."

"Ah, but we are and are not you."

"How con[ven]ient for you."

"You have no idea."

"Not even [the] part of [me th[at] ha]ppens to be part of you?

"I'm sorry, were you saying something?"

"Tell me, me and not-me, [wh]at's the endgame here?"

"You shall have to meet him."

"Who?"

"I'm sorry, your blah-blah-blah dillydallying chit-chatter game is used up. Let's go boys."

And a little incarnation in the wall right in front of Guy snapped his fingers. The hundreds of other Guys shrank in size, and sang different selections from the Guy Psycho songbook, creating a sonic wall of gibberish.

"That's [just] wrong," said Guy. "I [don't] sound like that at all!"

↑ I don't sound like that tall ↓

∞ I dune sounds like that fall ∞

≠ *I no sound like tramadol* ≠

⊗ I donna sound like drat no how ⊗

✱***I sound unlike this and that and this*** ✱,
said the little Guys.

"That's real mature," Guy said, tapping his foot on
the LCD floor, quavering the little Guy's voice down
there. All of the tiny avatars morphed into series of giant
close-ups of Guy's black lips, which ceased parroting his
own phrase, slowing down into a silent, stern pout.

"That's [bet]ter," said Guy.

"The humanoid," said the mouths.

"Hmmm?" asked Guy.

"Destroy!" said the mouths, zooming out to become
Guy Psychos again.

And then the maze was quiet. Guy turned around.
An angry red globe bopped towards him, across the
LCD floors. Guy's wingtips sprinted up the corridor, his
arms pumping, his hands slicing the air, the sides of his
jacket peeling away from his dark blue shirt as a thousand
Guy Psychos poured themselves into a thousand
microphones in a thousand different suits. Guy heard
the red sphere's grinding chortles storming through the
television corridor through the confusion of himselves.
He couldn't outrun the thing. He turned to face it, this
red ball of radiation with a breathing, chomping maw,
bopping towards him. Guy halted, turned, planted his
feet, and smashed the red orb in its electrified jaws,
sending it somehow bouncing back through the maze
of monitors. The millisecond of contact felt like icy-hot
carbonated jelly passing through his entire body. All the
little Guys went mum.

"Don't," said Guy, "do th[a]t again, whatever the Hell
that was."

A million Guy Psychos sulked. Silence.

A ringing came from his trouser pocket. Guy pulled a battered phone out and put the sliver of the receiver to his ear.

"Boss," said Lulu, "we need to be on the lookout for the Bull of Heaven."

"The Bull of Heaven?"

"It is a half-man, half bull—"

"A minotaur?"

"Well, you see, the Bull of Heaven is—okay, a minotaur, but with wings. Tiny wings."

"And you know we'll see this because?"

"The next tablet is when Gilgamesh and Enkidu face off against—"

"Gotcha."

And all the screens on the floor and walls showed cuneiformations that lead Guy on their dusty, misty path towards two *massive* doors.

Chapter 9:
The Bullfight of Heaven

When Guy arrived at the threshold, he was met by two bearded brutes wearing Assyrian sandals, sheepskin skirts, and turbans made from moray eels. The guards leaned the fleshy cushions of their bellies against their lancets, in a tableau of laziness that Wog and Wonk would have corrected out of nothing more than sheer pride in their calling.

"Hi th[ere]," said Guy, smiling big.

"English is *such* a barbaric tongue," complained Brute Number One.

"No wonder his lips have turned black," added Brute Number Two. "How *does* he say those words."

"Even in English," interrupted Guy, "there is such a thing as manners."

"No need to get sensitive," said Brute Number Two.

"My goodness m[e]—*me*, sensitive? That's a first."

"Look, all I'm saying is—you do talk a little—"

"Tch! So what is on the [other s]ide of that door— some gladiatorial horror-show in which I must cavort with a [mon]ster armed with scant [mo]re than a toothpick?"

"I'd *so* buy a ticket to that," said Brute Number One, whose sweaty turban puckered its lips.

"Well wh[a]t, then, are you guarding [the] threshold of?"

"I couldn't say," answered Brute Number Two.

Guy gritted his teeth until they creaked. "Might I be allowed, say, *in?*" he managed to ask, seething.

"That depends, you. Are you on the list?"

"What list?"

"*The* list."

"My name is Guy Psycho."

"Really?" asked Brute Number Two.

"Indeed, I [thi]nk so," said Guy.

"Right-o," said Brute Number One, pulling a tablet and reading glasses out from his sheepskin. "Peterson, Primrose, yes: *Psycho*—plus seventeen. Shall they be along later?"

"Yep."

"In with you, sir."

And the brute swung the door wide. Guy stared into the opening, blinking his black eyelids, and then stared back at the maze corridor, whose televisions were now inscribed with cuneiform. He couldn't read the characters, but he saw that they were spinning like a slot machine. So he walked between the corpulent guards, through the tall open doors, which creaked closed behind him.

Once inside, a parallelogram of luminescent aqua stretched for hundreds of feet, the discombobulating surface fretted with splashing, frolicking, dripping women in bikinis of every color of the spectrum. In the center of the pool was a Botticelli clamshell where a beatnik girl lay stomach-down reading *Guy Psycho and the Geodesic Ceiling of Forever*, her black Cons eddying in the air. She raised her horn-rims to eye Guy a moment, sighed, adjusted her silver bra-strap, and returned her attention to the book splayed in her hand.

Guy stumped inside, found a chaise lounge beside the water, and collapsed in an exhalation of joy. He popped off his wingtips and wiggled the big gold toe of his black socks, his arms slack at his sides.

"Some codeine and Chablis, Mr. Psycho?" said a voice hovering over a pewter tray with the proffered items on it.

"Is this Heav[e]n?"

"I *think* it is one of them, sir."

It was Reginald, Mr. Youngerman's valet. "Say—"

"Sir?"

"[I]s this all some sort [of] put on?"

"Put on?"

"You know—a pr[a]ctical joke."

"What do you mean, sir?"

"I mean," said Guy, swallowing the codeine, "I have very little idea how I got here, but [I] have even much *less* an idea how you've managed it."

"The house is rather mysterious, Mr. Psycho."

"I can see that," said Guy, letting the Chablis sluice down his almost golden throat. "Reginald," he said, "might you have a flare gun on you?"

"Mmnnnn, flare gun, sir?" said Reginald, patting a gloved hand upon either side of his tailcoat. "Ahhh," he said, yanking out an oversized red pistol, "here you are!"

Guy set down the wine glass upon the silver tray and took the gun from him. "Reginald, is there *more* of that Chablis?"

"I expect so, sir."

"G[ood]," said Guy, shooting a firework up into the black night sky. "Do have [a] look and bring as much as you can back," he added, dropping the flare gun onto the platter, "or a n[ip] of something else, if there happens to be no m[ore] of that."

"Very good, sir," said Reginald. "Silenus himself is envious of my master's wine cellar."

"Do you mean that literally, or—*never mind.*"

Guy plucked out his cell phone again and speed-dialed Lulu.

"Yeah, boss?" she said through a cacophony of static.

"Did you see that?"

"I did."

"That's wh[ere] I'm at. Some sort of f[a]b party. Wh[y] not come over, and bring the others you've found."

"We're on our way. Just remember *not* to—"

"That's fine, kitten. S[ee] you when you arrive. Tell the lugs out fro[nt] you're with *me*." And he closed the phone.

"Aren't you going to swim?" cooed a dreamy naiad.

Guy clutched at the bandage around his throat. "Alas and crap, no," he said, slouching over to the pool's lip and seating himself right over the water, "but I [am] pleased to make your lubricious acquaint[a]nce. Guy Psycho, Esquire."

A cool, wet, slender hand enwrapped his. "Lilith," the woman said, swirling her toes in the illuminated water. She giggled at him, loosening the curly locks of her hair, a delicious uncurling by the dimple of her fair chin, and over the naked curve of her shoulder, until the blonde filaments spread out across the illuminated blueness of the water.

"That's a w[o]nderful bathing suit you're almost not w[e]aring."

"This old thing?"

"Mmmhhmm. Why n[o]t tell me your life story, Lilith?"

"But my life is *not* a story, Mr. Psycho."

"Ah, Lilith, do call me Guy."

"Guy."

"That's bett[e]r. Do you like the party?"

"I'm starting to like it now," said Lilith, embracing the rim of the pool with her arms.

"What was wr[on]g with it before?"

"Well, for one thing, the girl-boy ratio was off."

"Fair enough," Guy said—*he* was the only male guest in attendance.

"And for another thing, there is, like, no music."

"A palpable min[u]s, I do confessit."

"And the host—well, he can be a bit touchy."

"Wh[oooo] issssss theee hhhhhost?" slurred Guy, for the Chablis and the codeine seemed to be forming a paste of his central nervous system, clogging his brain, making his tongue feel slug-like inside his mouth.

"I don't recall his name," Lilith said, rubbing her moist cheek against Guy's hand.

"But aaaa—big—ummmm—guy," said Guy, with some effort.

"Sure," said Lilith.

Another pewter tray descended down into his vision. Lilith plucked a glass from it, and so did Guy. "Cheers!" she said, clinking crystal. "Cheeeeers!" said Guy, again letting the liquid flow into himself in one motion.

"You sure can hold your liquor, Guy."

"Thannnnk you l[a]rge, Lilly. Tends to make the edge recede."

Lilith sprang upwards from the water, her hands gripping the indigo tile of the deck, her arms flexing, and kissed Guy's blackened, full lips. His black eyelids fluttered shut. Time ticked on.

It occurred to him that the soft passion of her kiss was no longer meeting his own, and he opened his eyes wide. Lilith was not there, but splashing to the other side of the pool. He was leaning over the agitated, shiny water. And he felt *something* like a hoof upon his shoulder.

"Who said this man could drink?" asked a voice behind him.

"I don't want [a]ny trouble," sighed Guy, rotating around slowwwwly.

Long-curving horns swooped over Guy's forehead. The bull-man's massive, muscular torso nearly concealed the tips of his miniature wings. The creature's wide, bovine snout was close to Guy's own face, and the downy fur looked uncanny, in combination with human eyes.

"Where art thine people?" gruffed the Bull of Heaven."

"They arrrrre en r[ou]te," answered Guy. "Nice Chablis, fella."

"Thank you," the Bull of Heaven beamed.

"No, thank y[ou]," insisted Guy.

"Still," said the Bull of Heaven, "you are showing a ton of nerve showing up here, and imbibing."

"It's [my] only vice," said Guy. "It's [one o]f my only vices."

"Please, sir," said a tugging at his cuff.

"What?" Guy said.

Pygmies in royal livery escorted Guy to a grand pavilion, where a pristine field sparkled in the bright moonlight. A grandstand, covered in lavender and cream-colored fabric, arose fifty feet into the air, and stretched along the green turf for a hundred feet. A crowd murmured to its seats. Guy was led to one end of the field, behind a Chinese screen, where a squire awaited him by a bench lined with various gleaming shapes of steel. "If you would remove your suit, sir," said the teenage boy, "I can get you fixed up here."

"Is this n[o]rmal for one of your mast[e]r's parties?" Guy asked, slipping off his dinner jacket.

"No," the squire admitted, squeezing iron pieces over Guy's shoulders. "Normally, he just shoots men in the stomachs."

"Ah, well that's go[od], but you [see], we have a show to put on—"

"Please stick your arm out, sir."

"And—ah, here you [go]—so I, and my [pe]ople, musn't stay but make our—"

"Now your other arm, please."

"Ouch."

As the squire ratcheted metal onto Guy's muscles with a wrench, Guy gazed up over the top of the screen into the stands. He squinted into the chattering crowd until he discerned, in the uppermost row, Lilith's figure in a little black dress. She wore a black veil that ruffled down her forehead, and drooped its mesh beneath her cheekbones, just above her lips. Lilith stood next to the entirety of his entourage, who looked quite revived with drinks in their hands. Concetta saluted him with an amber goblet of *something* and that pouting smirk of a smile. All of his people were slouched next to what was, Guy presumed, the Bull of Heaven's family. For minotaurs, he had to acknowledge, the family looked tremendous. Trudy waved at him. He held his hand up in recognition. "I'm going t[o] die," he said.

"Buck up, Sir Psycho—should be a fantabulous show," said the squire, his pageboy bobbing as he winched some lobster-looking metallic component to Guy's feet.

"Please, call me Guy."

"Certainly, Sir Guy."

Guy eyed the opposite end of the field, where there was a tent with steam unfurling from the seams. "What's Mr. Bully doing in th[e]re?" asked Guy.

"You don't want to know."

"Really?" Guy said, his head tilting—and then, from the valet stand, his dinner jacket trilled. The squire removed the phone from Guy's jacket, and handed it to him. "Yeah, Lulu," Guy drawled into the receiver.

"Isn't this great?" she said, her voice crisp.

"I don't supp[o]se you want to come over here?"

"You're doing great."

"*Get* your hinder ov[e]r here and bring—"

"So after you've killed him—"

"[Me], kill him?"

"—just remember to *not* do what Enkidu did after he and Gilgamesh killed the Bull of Heaven."

"Does your mother know you split [i]nfinitives?"

"Did I really split an infinitive? Actually, Mother thinks she is an acorn."

"I am stu[nned]."

"Look: this is important. *After* Enkidu and the Big G killed off your opponent, Enkidu cut off the thigh of the monster and threw it at Ishtar."

"And you thought *my* mann[e]rs were bad. [Why] would he do a thing like that?"

"Ishtar tried to woo or otherwise seduce Gilgamesh after his victory."

"So Enkidu threw m[ea]t?"

"When the tablet says that he threw the thigh, I think the scribe was being euphemistic for something *close* to the thigh."

"Ummmmmm."

"Yeah."

"So you're say[ing] I shouldn't do that?"

"Yes."

"Can I ask you s[o]mething?"

"Shoot, boss."

"Why do you think o[ne] of my first imp[ulses] might *ever* be to—"

"It's not you, Guy. It's the story."

"Thanks for the ch[a]t, *mon chat*," he said, pinching the phone closed, and handing it to the butler. Reginald had Guy's immaculate suit on a valet stand, and was brushing it. The squire upheld a helmet topped with what appeared to be a hood ornament of Guy in this armor, in which, atop the miniature helmet of the hood ornament, was a small protuberance that looked like an even smaller likeness of himself in this preposterous armor, and upon the tiny helmet of that there happened to be a microscopic—

"Um," said Guy.

The squire plopped the steel shell over Guy's face,

and then pulled it down, scraping the cheeks of Guy's large head. Reginald stalked forward, his red Van Dyke beard cocked at a contemplative angle. "There," he said, yanking the helmet two inches to the left, "this shall do." Guy looked out of the open visor, which blocked his periphery. He looked down at the armor.

Guy seemed to be wearing chrome garbage cans on his forearms, while metallic gargoyles seemed to be devouring his pectorals; surely an antique shop or thrift store somewhere had been robbed. He struggled to walk, or breathe for that matter, amidst all that claustrophobic tin.

"If I [o]nly had a heart," muttered Guy.

Clank, clank, clank! went the crowd.

Guy creaked over to the squire. "So," he asked, "which is my weapon[ry]?"

"Weaponry, Mr. Psycho?"

"I don't like the notion either, but th[a]t bugger seems dangerous."

"Ummmm."

"Are there any weapons?"

"I'm just an armorer's son," said the squire.

Mariachi horns blazoned the start of the tourney. Guy smiled at the crowd. Amidst the clamor, Lilith descended to the front of the grandstand. She crooked a heel into the railing, unclasped the strap that encircled her ankle, and dropped the black pump to the floor. Then, she reached her hand down her thigh, and curled a black stocking down her creamy skin.

The crowd *oohed*.

Lilith unfurled the silk over the railing, and let go, the hosiery drifting in the balmy night. The squire snagged the limp limb from the air and over-handed it to the metal flange of Guy's elbow. Guy kissed his gauntleted hand, and swung his arm in a squeaky gesture of loving salute.

Reginald proffered another Chablis, which Guy gulped down. Then Guy returned his smile to the heaving pavilion, bowing in his itchy metal skin. Reginald clanked down the visor, reducing Guy's vision even more. From between slits, the squire hastened out of his periphery.

The Bull of Heaven whooshed out of his tent, magnificent, muscular, ripped. Guy bowed, and the minotaur nodded, a big, brass ring swinging from his septum. Then the half-man, half-bull crouched into the grass, his human feet digging in, his loincloth swaying, his hooves planted ahead of him, his horns glistening out of his terrible head, his little wings atwitter. Hot steam tunneling from his glistening nostrils deliquesced blades of grass.

Guy set down one foot, flexing his legs, inclining far forward, but just couldn't help himself—and jive-danced up and down the fairground, watusi-ing in his steel shell, wobbling his steel shoes in the mashed potato, flashing his arms like a monkey, and then, after much twitterpation, set down one foot, flexing his legs, inclining far forward, saying to himself, "I'm so pretty."

The Bull of Heaven's eyes glowed red, his sneer uncovering vicious mandibles that grated upon each other with spine-chilling effect.

The light-post went red-red-*green*! and the two combatants hazarded down the pavilion's center into each other's way. The thousand-fold spectators suspended their collective breath as the Bull of Heaven's low, uncanny stride seemed to be carried up by the hummingbird volition of its wings, while Guy's tramping appeared even more drunken than it was—no one should ever have to sprint in armor—so that the Man staggered far off the path to one side, and then careered off to the other side, so that the Bull of Heaven himself had to angle his way down the rut of the fairgrounds and then counter that adjustment with another as Guy moved, so that the angles were not aligned when the two bodies met: Guy glanced the Beast's face with a drop-kick, sending the singer's body into a horizontal whirl that bore a Guy-sized circle into the turf with an eardrum-imploding jangle; in the same instant, the Bull of Heaven's massive momentum dragged him five rows up into the stands.

The cheers were shrill as the beast clambered down back onto the field and the arm of a crane eased down to pluck Guy from the ground. The senneteers blew *La Cumparsita* over the screams as the squire swept Guy's hodgepodge of armor clean of grass and dirt. Someone in the front row taunted the Bull of Heaven, and was summarily gored. Guy resumed his stance, and then was turned by the squire towards the center of the fairground. The Beast flicked his wings, then crouched down into a taut readiness. The beast stared fiery-eyed at the Man, and the Man stared at the striped reality of the beast through his steel visor.

The crowd lulled. Red—red—green! went the light, and vroom went the Bull of Heaven, and "Giddy up!" went Guy in a stagger towards the amalgamated blur hurtling at him.

When Guy came to, armor littered the fairground. He lay in a stupor, legs akimbo, in his hula maiden boxers. The squire and other liveried pygmies dusted him off with little brooms, closed his legs together, taped his ribs. Then they winched him into an upright posture, erected a Chinese screen, and dosed him with smelling salts as they put his suit back on him. Meanwhile, the Bull of Heaven was once more extricated from the framework of the pavilion.

"Regin[ald]," said Guy, "can I have a little more of that ambrosial wh[atev]er it is?"

"Certainly, Mr. Psycho. It shall be a moment as I open a bottle."

In a nanosecond the Chinese screen was shredded and Guy was mid-air, his back pressed to the minotaur's forehead. The Man's bulk was wedged between those sublime angus horns. The Bull of Heaven jabbed his spikes into the ground. Guy sprang his body over the beast's back and grabbed its meaty tail.

"Don't do that," intoned the Bull of Heaven.

"You ch[ea]ted," warbled Guy.

"So?"

"So I'm not letting go."

The Bull of Heaven stared at Guy in great perplexity, chewing on his lower lip.

"Come on, leggo!" shouted the minotaur.

"So, you surrender then?" asked Guy.

Guy was whooshed around behind the minotaur, who try as he might couldn't quite catch the part of himself that Guy held, around and around and around in whooshes of ancient dust. "H[o]w's—my—drink?" asked Guy, in minute distortions of voice.

Reginald held the Chablis between his knees, his fist straining around the corkscrew. "It is reluctant to yield its cork, sir," said the valet.

"Here, all[ow] me," said Guy, stepping aside to set the bottle between his own thighs while the Bull of Heaven ran around in circles by himself. Guy clutched the bottle-opener in his fingers, and eased his arm back and exhaled, once, twice, three times—the Beast coming to a stop, shaking his head, then sprinting at Guy—and with a guttural grunt the Man yanked the corkscrew out of the cork, his body collapsing backward. The twist of steel was held over his head until it met the Bull of Heaven's skull with such impact that it imbedded there—deeply—between the Beast's eyes. The Chablis spouted from the half-ruptured cork.

Guy stood up, brushed off his clothes, and gazed upon the corpse of the Bull of Heaven.

The grass withered.

The telephone rang.

Chapter 10:
Zeal Without Knowledge

"Lulu?"

"I am *not* a Lulu."

"Are you animal, mineral, or—ummmm—g[o]ddess?"

"You're not so stupid as your looks."

"Thank you large."

"Don't chatter," she said, static frothing over the dulcetest voice, "your satellites will not hold up under all this astronomical strain." The last of the grass was receding into the earth, as if vacuumed from underneath.

"Spe[ak]."

"None of your friends are going to do something rude?"

Guy eyed Philippe far up in the pavilion, where the bassist was cramming a snozzbery-covered funnel cake into his mouth. A throng jostled around him, flowing down to the fairgrounds.

"Negatory," said Guy, "I pr[omi]se."

"I'm losing reception."

"It might just be my v[oice]."

"You are a singer?"

"Sort of."

"Never mind. Are you willing to—"

The black sky was crisp, punctuated with tiny white embers, until a scrim of cloud passed across the moon and gloomed the pavilion.

"The answer [is] yes."

"But—"

"The answer is yes, I'll bring the tablet—but [I will] need a ride, *and* a map."

"You have the tablet, then?"

"Mark its location [on] the map."

"It shan't be easy for you."

"It never is."

"You've done this before?"

"I d[on']t know."

A pop and a squealing signaled the grand pavilion's implosion. Guy's entourage sauntered over, as the other spectators disappeared into the blue mist.

"Ish?" Guy said, but the line was silent. The phone slid into his jacket pocket.

"What now?" said Lulu.

"We move," said Guy.

"How?"

A crane maneuvered a long, massive crate before them. The words LARABEE INDUSTRIES, INC. stretched diagonally across aged wood, which thumped down onto the earth. Two pygmies atop the crate jimmied open the end with long, gleaming crowbars.

The darkness inside the tremendous box emitted an abrupt, deep-throated huff.

"Whatcha think it is?" asked Blee, bracing himself behind Simone's glistening petticoats.

Aurora clicked her flashlight and swept the beam inside. Two gigantic Lipizzaners emerged out of the wooden container in a seismic clatter, tugging forth a lapis lazuli chariot that stretched thirty-five feet. With a petulant whinny, the beasts seized the quavering muscles of their legs to a halt.

"From strange to stranger," said Trudy, with a toothy smile. "It's ultramatic."

"What's the matter?" Trudy asked Archibald, who clutched her shoulder, hard. Sweat dripped from his brown curls.

"Not fond of horses," he said. "I *still* have saddle sores from when I was fifteen."

"Now, now, now," said Trudy, caressing the shoulder of his Colin McFeeny dinner jacket, "That's all in your head."

In a swish of torn modular satin, Lulu knelt by the cart. She pulled her auburn bangs from her face, the tips scraping her glittering cheekbones. Her glossy lips pouted as she traced the lapis lazuli, embossed *tableaux* that arose from the mottled blue stone. There was Enkidu in pornographic dalliance with Ishtar's harlot. A diminutive Gilgamesh mourned his friend. Odysseus nabbed Achilles in drag. Grendel snuffed it. Loki drove the clouds mad. Cleopatra breastfed a famished asp. Lulu's knees shuffled on the ground, following the sculpture's progress along the chariot. Who engraved this? she thought, these images more distinct than reality itself, even in this darkness. The blue surface seemed to glow from within. And the scenes segued one to the next, linking Apollo 11, mammoth hunts, faery orgies, panoramic wars, Lulu's own father six leagues below Belgrade, a diminutive incarnation of herself kneeling by a stretch chariot, and *then* upon the rear of the actual the chariot ("Lulu?") there was Guy, figured in a long robe, his eyes black even in lapis lazuli, his tiny gaze lost in a shock corridor that became the entire opening of the back of the chariot. The real Guy had spent a decade in the sanitarium before going pro. It had never been any of their business. Was this little Guy *blinking* at her? He looked so very impossibly sad.

"Earth to Lu[lu]," said Guy.

"Huh?" she said.

"Shall we g[e]t a move on? Do we need this frieze?"

"We can go," she said, not moving.

"Is there a m[ap in] there? Lulu, pay attention, so we can bustle."

Lulu tucked the collar of her black leather jacket into her nape, and looked up at her boss, unable to speak or move, but gazing into his blank eyes.

Simone came out of the crate with a seven-foot cylinder clutched in her arms, a diagonal slash emerging from the lathery fluff of her petticoats.

"Map," pointed Guy with two fingers, and Lulu walked in her black motorcycle boots over to where Archibald and Trudy splayed the massive paper.

"Ahem," coughed Lulu. The background of the map was gray, and had a single dot that read "You are here," and an X hovering off the edge of the world that read: "The thirteenth tablet is here."

"Whatever happ[ened] to plain-old latitude and longitude?" groused Guy. A black grid emerged on the map, and then nameless topographies bled onto the paper, topographies that shifted, evolved, and swirled, the Euphrates throbbing like the spasmodic vein of a hangover.

Lorrie looked at the map, then at the landscape, then at the map again. She measured out the distance on the map with an arm's length, then looked up at the landscape. She looked back down at the map, whose image was once again turning, like a compass that couldn't find north. "How do we get to X?" she yowled. "Our destination is still rather vague, without a name or a legend or even images that will stand still!"

"I know how to get there," said one of the horses.

"Listen to that!" said Blee.

"I speak better than *you* do," said the horse.

"Ahoy!" said Guy, "Why didn't you [clue] us earlier about this, pal o' min-o?"

"Why did you presume I couldn't talk?"

"I didn't presume that. I pr[e]sumed you didn't know

the answer."

The horse huffed, gazing into the middle distance.

"Great steed, will y[ou] please take us there?" pleaded Guy. "The chariot and you look amazing. It would be a shame not to take a ride."

"All get aboard, if you please."

The entourage filed onto the lapis lazuli. "Alexis," said Guy, "your equestrian expertise is required up front." Alexis slipped between Simone and Archibald. Her little black crinoline dress swished with even the smallest motion of her muscles. Her thick-heeled Mary Janes clunked on the ultramarine marble floor of the chariot. She smoothed a dark finger wave from her brow and clutched the reins. "Okay now," she said, "Gee'yup!"

The pair of horses strained at the ground, hooves grooving the yellow earth, until the long chariot budged, the spokes of the wheel squeaking a slow revolution. They accelerated in spastic jerks, as the steeds worked to attain a steady volition, which they soon did. And then, as their progress under the stars became observable, the volition *continued* to increase, and then continued, and continued. The stars overhead quivered and wept and the chariot lurched in a gush of movement, and then another lurch, and another and another and the spokes blurred and another lurch, and the dreamscape plowed by them in microconsciousness as they clutched each other's limbs. And then the chariot rose.

Icy gravity distended into their bodies, and their own thrombotic brains were reduced to ocular sensations so that their own screams went indiscernible among the specks of wind. With another lurch, their vehicle defined a faltering arc heaving over the land, the sky, the very void of wherever they were. Vinyl-looking feathers flapped from the back of one of the horses. The huge wings whuffed at the atmosphere. Then—with a jerking jerk—the whole raving inertia stuttered so that the axis of the chariot slowwwwwwwwly drifted onto its left side. "Only one of these horses has wings," Alexis managed to shout, the whole off-kilter shebang falling.

Chapter 11:
The Jinni Who Dreamed in Flesh

The trajectory deteriorated with each gallop. In a few moments, they would be spiraling straight down.

"Did *no* one notice that [one] of these horsies was *not* like the other?" screamed Guy.

"You didn't notice, either!" Simone said.

The winged Lipizzaner turned his massive head, his white mane frizzing, and gazed back over his withers at Guy, appearing to raise one horsy eyebrow

"Right!" said Guy. Guy studied the locomotion ahead. Simone's blond hair fluttered his cheek. He put one wingtip on the front of the chariot, clutched Simone's shoulder, and then leaped forward onto the torso of the wingless steed. Guy gesticulated into the wind with one hand, the other trying to cradle the horse's neck.

"What *is* he doing?" asked Lorrie, sliding into Aurora and twirling against Vernita.

"Don't interrupt," said Blee, who braced a leg against the side of the chariot in an attempt to stay inside. "I watched him do this once in Atlantic City."

Guy managed to snatch the reins from the air and yank them. Their momentum jolted backwards, slipping into a dizzying, centripetal spin. Lulu clutched the rim of the chariot. Pasha whooshed by. The sandy air screamed.

Lulu looked down, seeing nothing. If we keep falling, she thought, and there is nothing beneath us, then what danger is there, except an eternity of falling?

Whump! went the soft, black soil of nothingness.

Guy and his palomino were half-submerged in loam. The Postmodernaires landed totteringly on their feet. Archibald, quite pale, shivered in the middle of the chariot. The musicians were flounced over fifty yards.

Guy squeezed up out of the silt, which granulated off of his clothes without him even having to brush the fabric. Behind him, the Lipizzaners clambered whitely out from the dirt. "Ahem," said a voice behind Guy.

Guy twisted around, and recoiled.

Alone in the dark, askew in a canvas chair, a man with the elongated face of a baboon played the blues on a lyre, using the stem of a palm frond as a slide. A messenger bag dangled from the baboon-man's leather girdle. His big toe rutted the dirt.

"My grandm[o]ther warned me about p[eople] like you," said Guy.

The jinni looked down its long purple nose at him, and then offered a gruff snort.

("Louis Pr[i]ma, patron saint of interspecies relations, guide me," Guy whispered to himself.)

"Guy," said Lulu, grabbing his huge hand. "Let's find out what he wants."

"Good p[lan]," said Guy.

Arm-in-arm, they approached the seated creature. Everyone crowded in behind them.

"Halloo," said Guy.

"Hi," said the man with a baboon's elongated face.

"My name is Guy Psycho, esquire. And you are?"

"Shaytoom."

"It's a pleas[ure,] Shay."

The jinni nodded.

"So, my dear Shay," continued Guy, "I [can't h]elp but notice that [you h]appened to be chilling far off the beaten path."

"Indeed."

"Were you waiting [for] us?"

"That might be difficult to say."

"Shay, what [do] you want? What's th[is] all about? Why are you here?"

"I could," said the jinni, "ask the same of you."

"We are trying [to] get to X-marks-the-spot, if you *must* know."

"But why get to X?" asked the jinni, strumming a minor chord on his lyre.

"We [are] trying to save the world."

"*Your* world, you mean?"

"That's the one. Now, why are [*you*] here?"

"Hold on, it will come to me."

An eternal minute passed, the jinni gnawing the end of the palm leaf, as if for some mnemonic boost. Lorrie thought of the perfect choreography for *Breaking Love*. Pasha thought of playing in the snows of St. Petersburg. Archibald thought of a vivid dream he once had about losing all his teeth at a circus in Dayton, Ohio.

"Ah," said the jinni. "His Royal Highness—"

"You mean Gilgamesh?"

"—has asked me to appear here to deliver a message to you."

"[And]?"

"And what?"

"The [mess]age?"

"Ah, so: You will not find your thirteenth tablet until *he* gets what he wants first."

"And what does he—"

"His Royal Magisterial Extraordinariness *wants* what was taken from him so very long ago: the very fruit of youth."

"This sounds naughty," said Aleister.

"Look, mister," said Guy, "we're [in] a quite rather humongous hurry."

"I think you'll find," said the jinni, "that the most difficult way in this world is always the easiest, and almost always the fastest."

Guy stared up into the blackest sky. The jinni looked up, too.

"What are you looking at?" the jinni asked.

"Really, really long marionette str[ing]s," Guy said. "Lulu, parse this, ummm, man's [dem]and, please."

"After Enkidu passed on, Gilgamesh was inconsolable. He wandered the wilderness, becoming less civilized, becoming like a beast, like his friend Enkidu was, before he was civilized by love. Eventually, the madness of the king passed, but his sorrow would not, so Gilgamesh tried to appease his sadness with action. He crossed the River of Death seeking the only man who survived the great flood of old."

"Uh oh," said Guy.

"Gilgamesh meets the ancient man, who promises to tell Gilgamesh the secrets of longevity if he can pass the test of endurance, to stay awake for a week's time. Gilgamesh fails the test, sleeping for many days after the exhaustion of his journey."

"I know what that f[eels] like," said Guy.

"Gilgamesh is heartbroken again, returning to the facts of his own mortality, and his infinite loneliness without his friend. The survivor of the great flood takes pity on this king, and instructs him in how to retrieve the prickly fruit of the gods, that will allow him to live forever among mankind."

"Sounds [li]ke a mai tai at the Jetsetter Lounge," said Guy.

Lulu said, "Gilgamesh was successful in retrieving the Fruit of Life, as it is sometimes called. However, a river snake stole the fruit of everlasting life while Gilgamesh slept on his way back to Babylonia."

"The man slept a lot [on] the job."

"The job's harder than it looks," said the jinni.

"Fair enou[gh]," said Guy. "And if we fetch this p[ri]ckle pear, we can then advance unmolested towards the thirt[eenth] tablet?"

The baboon lips of the jinni pursed. "Bringing it back shan't be easy," he said.

"If one mo[re pe]rson tells me that, I am going to milk a bicycle," said Guy. "So [where] do we find this fruit?"

"What's wrong with your voice?" asked the jinni.

"Please try to foc[us]: prickly pear? Wh[e]re?"

"With the snake, of course."

"Still?"

"Still!"

Guy sighed, his black eyelids shut. "So wh[e]re is this snake?"

"At the bottom of the stream."

"What stream?"

But before the jinni answered, the rude gurgle of rushing water was audible. Everyone looked behind them to see a greenish smear of liquid churning through the black soil of nothingness. Guy scooped up the map from where it had landed on the ground and gazed at the parchment: across all that abysmal geography, there was the river, squirming. Its far western tail curled and uncurled around an icon of a prickle pear.

"What's [this] *really* about?" asked Guy.

The jinni was mum.

Guy brought the map over to the winged horse. "Say, Fireball, can w[e get] to this point?"

"I think so, yes," said the horse, his wings waving.

"Safely?" asked Guy.

"Sure," said the horse.

"Alexis," said Guy, "my bluegrass angel, I presume you have some idea how to harness these beasties?"

"I'm not a farmer, Guy, but I'll see what I can do," she said, checking the harnesses, and making some adjustments. As the others clambered aboard, she rubbed the undersides of the horses' jaws with both hands. Instead of a thin layer of fuzziness, she felt a texture that seemed like plastic. Two shiny wings fluttered. She opened her mouth, looked at Guy at the front of the chariot, and then shut her mouth. "No," she thought, "let this go." She stuck her big, black Mary Jane into the spokes of one of the front wheels, and swished up over the railing into the front of the chariot. Guy yielded her the reins. She snapped the straps, a sound that, combined with the shushing of her black crinoline, sounded like the single shake of a maraca. The chariot jolted forth, sending up shadows across the jinni's seated, smiling form. They pulled alongside the glowing river, and then swerved, plunging into the water.

"Bye, bye," said the jinni, waving, and then plucking more music from his lyre.

Chapter 12:
The Serpent of Youth

The liquid propulsion of the river looked dangerously green as it poured over the sides of the chariot. The horses, the lapis lazuli, and the band kept sinking (down, down, down) until submerged, and *surging* ever forward. Gelatinous, the molten amethyst water pressed against their clothes and flesh. Their progress disrupted a school of fish, glinting silver and scattering. Guy wondered how fish could stand it, and for an entirety of a lifetime, too! But soon he had to wonder how long *he* could stand it. The greenness brightened so bright that Guy shoved Wayfarers over his eyes.

That was better. The walls of this riverbed were round, and ridged, and swerved before his very tired eyes. Aurora clung to his arm, and Alexis and Simone clung to her arms, and the pull of this interlocked entourage forced Guy to reach out for something to hold, or else they would all fall out of the chariot, be left behind, to drown in this horrible muck. Instead of the carved stone of the chariot railing, he felt something long and thick, like the end of a rope, although as his grip slipped he saw that it tapered at the end. Like the tail of a serpent. And the handhold Guy had seemed to be moving independently of the chariot. The water pulsed emerald and radioactive lime and then Guy saw a dark plane above them that grew lower the longer he looked at it. Guy felt a cool spot atop his cropped hair as the green liquid receded down his face, his body, and the giant, wobbly wheels of the slowing chariot.

Guy gasped an electric, broken wheeze. The Postmodernaires sucked in oxygen in hoarse, inhuman ululations. Philippe ignited a miraculously dry cigarette. Archibald patted Trudy on the back, as she coughed out green gooiness over the side of the lapis lazuli.

Guy let go, and something the size of the tunnel itself slithered out of view. Guy performed a headcount on the company: ... fifteen, sixteen, seventeen. That tally felt short to Guy—who was missing? Oh yes, *he* was the eighteenth. No panic. Cucumber City, him. So where was the prickly pear, or thorny gourd, or what have you?

"[L**lalul*!]" shrilled Guy, his fingers spasming at the Gaultier gauze encircling his throat.

The entourage stood stock-still.

Blee pressed through the others, hugged the boss. All the rest of the entourage saw was the drummer's thatch of bleached hair, the back of his sopping black suit, and Guy's shaky fingertips clamping across Blee's back. A minute later, Guy's trembling stopped. He sighed a moist, reluctant breath, then inhaled, his chest expanding his dripping chalk-stripe suit. Guy slipped his Wayfarers atop his frazzled black hair, and pinched Blee's face, and stepped off the chariot. Lulu transferred a moleskin notepad to Guy's hand, and then a fountain pen. He upheld the moleskin, scribbled something in it, and then showed it to Lulu, standing at his side.

Her eyes scanned Guy's scratchy scrawl, and then, lowering her voice and mimicking his Brahmin-laced slur, read: "Forthward!"

Guy smirked at her, his black lips pert, his eyes hard.

Sybil walked ahead, green muck smearing her diamond-encrusted pumps. With the elevation of her heels, she was two inches taller than Guy. With her slimed white dress gloves poised at her sides, she walked meticulously, although the segmented walls of this tunnel *moved*, and so did the spongy floor. What she wouldn't give for a Geiger counter.

The sounds of their walking had no echo, did not travel at all. The aural vacuum was like being in the studio. After the seventh bend of the tunnel, the Posmodernaires reached their stride, and stalked in unison, even without the metronome tock of their heels upon the ground. By the tenth, they sang, in dreamy syncopation:

Green as the sea
Alpha and omega of me

Blue as the sky
The pleasurous azure of why

    Waking in the morning, such a novel feeling
    So much more adoring, O so genteeling

    Disappearing agos, twinkling of starlight
    Tiny tomorrows, holding so tight

White as the dew
Latitude and longitude of you

Yellow as the sun
flaxen parallaxis of one

    Walking through forests, operas of pine trees
    Prismatic contests, muses of the breeze

    Brooks so glimmering, dancing of iris
    Birds so shimmering, taste of our bliss

Silver as the mist
The very round sound of exist

Pink as the gloam
Cool cartography of home

> Lounging beneath palms, sands at low tide
> Chant of cicada psalms, the ever of outside

> Soaring over the waves, liquescent speeding
> What the wing craves, liminal receding

Blue as the sky
The pleasurous azure of why

Green as the sea
Alpha and omega of me

The pathway opened upon a midway filled with gray-purple bunting, and a canvas banner stretching across the sky that read "Dreamland." The ground was covered in straw and sawdust. The calliope roared ancient dirges, and the sideshow promised grotesqueries in posters looming ten stories tall: there was a man-faced dog, a flea on that dog who could ski through the mind of an elderly weasel, and a thought of that weasel that could turn the whole world inside out. Guy and his companions all understood this, even though the captions underneath the massive charcoal illustrations appeared in cuneiform.

"I want a frosted nut log," said Trudy, as she rubbed her swollen ankles.

"We're getting further away," muttered Archibald.

"What now?" asked Lulu.

The ground lurched westward, snagged, and then a slithering swelling displaced the soil from the sawdust and hay. The tail of the serpent snapped out of the black, and then zoomed back below, a sine wave warping the earth, overturning kiosks and tents and the caravans of gray golem roustabouts.

"After it!" screamed Lulu, and the entourage rushed after the great wriggling of the hay, which stretched now for sixty or so feet.

"Is this a good idea?" asked Archibald, to which Trudy shrugged, which was not easy to do running at full speed. Guy ran ahead of them now, his big shoes kicking up in front of him, near the serpent's tail.

The thing zagged north, which caused Guy to stop. Wham! Simone knocked him over, and Lulu knocked her over, and Alexis knocked her over, and Blee knocked her over.

"Right foot red," said Lorrie to the prostrate tangle beneath her. And then Aleister knocked her over. The furrow of the earth receded out to a large, gray tent in the middle distance.

"You guys have your fun," said Aurora, "I am going to fetch our fruit of everlasting life."

Aurora looked back. Lulu examined the gauze around Guy's throat, trying to brush the dirt from the fabric. Simone touched a stain on Guy's shirt. Was that Vernita re-combing his hair? "Ahem!" Aurora yelled, one foot crooked in the ground, until everyone bustled forward again, towards the distant tent, with her. The entrance flaps were attached to two staffs, making an awning. Everyone stooped inside, into the dimness. The tallish ceiling of the tent drooped with lanterns fretted with the tremulous lights of fireflies. Aurora gazed up.

The great snake down-turned its head at them, in a sort of frown. "What sssort of busssnessss issss thissss?"

he asked, his tail curled about an orange spiky melon, a dead sun wrapped in barbed wire.

"Sir—" Lulu began.

"Like, we need that," said Aleister, as he pointed behind the beast.

"Thank you so much," said Lulu. "What my bright young fiend was trying to say—" she said, addressing the serpent.

"—issss that you need thisssss?" he asked, bandying the Fruit of Everlasting Life in his tail.

"Well, yessss," said Lulu.

"I ssssssee," he said.

A minute passed in stillest silence.

"And?" asked the serpent.

"Can we have it?" asked Lulu.

"Come and take it, missssss."

Lulu took a wary step in his direction. Guy clutched her arm, stopped her.

The serpent smiled wide, a wry line threatening to decapitate the sandy angles of his head. The black slits of his pupils swelled like glass muscles in the glittery yellow of his eyes. The Fruit of Everlasting Life gyrated around the gloomy air as he swept his tail around the interior of the tent.

"It isss too, too delicioussssss," he purred.

Lulu looked at Guy, whose eyes squinted blackly at this serpent. Yes, Guy had seen this before, or somehow *done* this before, this déjà vu scenario, or else it was Saint George or Sir Galahad or maybe King Gilgamesh himself, or Gilles de Reis or Sid Vicious or Guy's grandfather Seamus McConnelly, or Krazy Kat or Ulysses or Marilyn Monroe, or Caligula or John Dilinger or maybe it was him, or maybe it was his older self seeing him do this now, which somehow meant that he was going to survive this—unless he was wrong, and this sensation was an aftereffect of the infinity of pharmaceuticals he was given in the 1990s while a resident at St. Dymphna's.

No time to worry about that now. He must *become* his vision of himself. On the moleskin, Guy scrawled, "When I close his mouth, grab that blossom." He paced the line of them, showing the page to everyone, until one by one they nodded assent. He stepped in front of Philippe and Blee, and unfastened their belts before they could protest. (Philippe's trousers eased down his pale, thin legs, revealing silk Yo Bix™ boxers he had bought in Tokyo. Blee's checkered trousers stayed put on his meaty thighs.) Guy worked the tongue of one belt into the fastener of the other, and then slid the end of the second belt through the opening of the first, forming a lariat of leather draped in his open palm. Gritting his teeth through the snarl of his black lips, he approached the serpent.

The serpent chewed sideways a moment on its forked tongue. "Issss thissss how it'sssss going to be?" he asked, his pupils again narrowing to slits.

Guy's sneer turned into a black smile. The serpent's tail tightened around the fruit, the thorns ripping its skin. The fireflies screamed little screams.

Guy was in the darkened dust, just lunging out of the serpent's strike. A tent-pole snapped, and canvas sagged, lanterns jostling. Guy just managed to stand when the serpent darted again. Guy hopped back several feet, and when the serpent came up short, Guy kicked his snout, sending swirls of earth into the pits along the ridge of its head. The serpent recoiled into itself, scouring its face against the curves of its flesh, the skin shredding from the panicky friction.

Slithering sidelong towards Guy, the serpent no longer presented his head as a target. Guy had no means of escape as the segmented lengths of the serpent's fraying abs rammed Guy against the rippling wall of the tent.

"Hurry up, Guy!" said Simone.

Guy un-tucked the pocket square from his jacket front, wiped the blood from his nose. The serpent gyrated its abdominals once more. Guy kicked the parchment flesh with his size-14 wingtip. The serpent twisted its neck and swooped over Guy, who fell backwards and grabbed it by its lower jaw. The great snake uplifted its head high, crashing through the lanterns, Guy slipping. The serpent's chin crushed him into the ground. The beast uplifted the angry rhombus of its head. Guy lay motionless, entrenched in the earthen floor of the tent.

The serpent darted to strike—and froze. Two belts cinctured his mouth. The huge glinting yellow orbs of his eyes reflected Guy's face, two black smiles of eternal mockery. The serpent felt a tug, and glared back at its poor, gray tail. Lulu had removed her leather coat, and wrapped the Fruit of Everlasting Life it. She walked to the far side of the tent with the prize, the other women enclosing her. It was all over.

"[I'm gro]wing [used to th]is," said Guy, with a distinct crinkling of joints as he lurched from the crater-silhouette of himself. Blee and Aleister reached down their forearms, and Guy locked his with theirs, and was lifted up. Guy patted his cheeks, as if to check that his head was still there, and then ran his hands through his dark, cropped hair.

Before them, the serpent coiled, its ruined tail tattooing a rage into the earth. A film covered its brown skin. The serpent gazed at Guy's wingtips.

"[Easy now]," said Guy, as those wingtips stalked closer to it. The serpent peered upward through its own convolutions, expressionless, its throat pulsing.

"Guy, what are you doing?" said Simone.

"[I don't want] to [leave this] f[el]la defenseless."

"But boss—"

But the belts were already undone and tossed over Guy's shoulder.

"You are awfully trusssssting," said the serpent.

"Hey," said Guy, "Begone from [here]."

The snake unfurled himself in an explosion of reptilian essence, snapping more and more tent poles, the ceiling slumping, swinging lanterns into their heads.

"You people are not even ssssuposssssed to be here!"

"Go [shed your] skin!"

An undulant S made its slithery departure from the semi-demolished tent. "Give me a hand, everyone," said Aurora, who reached up and removed a lantern. All the others, except Lulu, who held the Fruit of Everlasting Life, collected the lanterns from the tent.

They emerged from the canvas flap with their arms full of these glass bowls, and then opened them, releasing the fireflies into the dark firmament, dots of ghostly light streaming up and up, joining their place with the other stars.

"So where do we take this Fruit?" asked Lulu, holding up the bundle in her coat.

"Ahem," whined the sky, and a constellation of embers formed an arrow pointing away from the fairgrounds.

"Imagine that!" said Pasha.

"Let's go, [kiddos]."

And so they trudged into the dunes, in a long, single-file. Trudy was the last in line, her eight-inch heels tiring her on the compacted sand. Somehow she got sand in her charcoal stockings. After several minutes of walking, she sensed a tap on her shoulder. She craned her head around, her black ringlets bouncing, to find that Archibald was now behind her.

"Whatever were you up to?" she asked.

"Needed to tie my shoes," he said.

"Really."

"Don't you trust me?"

"You're not entirely honest," she said, "but I trust you."

"Goody," said Archibald, "I think."

"Keep up, you two!" bellowed Simone ahead of them.

Trudy put her arm in his. "You raced back. You weren't even winded."

"Princeton track."

"Ah: so. And what were you doing back there?"

Archibald slipped something into her hand. She turned to the front and lifted her hand to her face. She held, in a swirl of wax paper, a frosted nut log.

Chapter 13:
The Thirteenth Tablet of *Gilgamesh*

They didn't have to walk far. Beneath the celestial arrow, the sandy landscape swelled up and swirled, a twisting, elevated catwalk above the dunes. The path then valleyed, winnowing down to a stepped crevasse, which approached a cave. Guy and his entourage clambered inside the whorl of stone. Inside, their path narrowed still more with a series of shadowy, throbbing stalagmites reaching up, as if to buttress the dark, red ceiling. Holding a candelabrum that shimmered with a dozen candle-flames, Reginald stood expectantly, all coattails and sleeked hair and official smile emerging from his pointy, red beard.

"Bravo, sir!" he said.

"Just [*who*] is it you are working for, Reg?" asked Guy.

"Mr. Youngerman's associates can be—well, I know," said Reginald, smiling, "this must seem rather irregular."

"Act[u]ally, [thi]s started irregular, and has become—"

"Madness," said Lulu.

"I know nothing about that, miss," said Reginald.

"What do we [do] now?"

"First, I recommend you leave that," said Reginald—gesturing with two fingers at the Fruit of Life in Lulu's arms—"with me."

"This needs to go to King Gilgamesh," she said, turning her bundle away from his glance.

"I would advise against that course of action, miss."

"Do [te]ll, Reg."

"If his Royal Highness were to acquire this Fruit of Life, he would, in fact, try to eat it."

"And?"

"The thorns alone would kill him."

"And w[e] care … why?" asked Guy.

"Mr. Youngerman would be disappointed should any harm come to his Royal Highness."

"Does anyone in [this]," Guy huffed, "consortium get along [and] cooperate?"

"Seldom, sir."

"Must be a right ass-pain for you."

Reginald offered a microscopic sniff. "Might I take possession of that for you?"

"We can't hand this over," said Lulu, switching the burden around to her hip, "without *first* being allowed to see the thirteenth tablet of *Gilgamesh*."

"Of course," said Reginald, "You will find it right through that door."

Guy sprinted, his meaty legs kicking high. He yanked with his large hands upon the ring of the door, until its stone weight gasped, and scraped open. On the other side was a vaulted, white room, lined by a row of white rectangular pedestals with the pristinest glass cases atop them. Inside each transparent cube, there was a brittle rounded clay slab inscribed with cuneiform.

The Postmodernaires counted the plaques, in ascending harmony: *x, xi, xii, xiii!* They sang the last the loudest. Fault-lines crept like sudden roots through the surface of the glass, until the transparent cubes imploded.

"Pardon, miss," said Reginald to Pasha, as he removed a dust-brush from his jacket pocket, and bristled and dabbed the thirteenth tablet clean of shards.

"What's it say?" Lorrie asked, the silhouette of her hair spiking onto the cuneiform.

Lulu stepped close to the tablet. This was going to be difficult. The inscription wasn't complete, for one thing, the text was a peninsula of words eroding from the edges of the stone, and text was chipped through the middle, too, in reservoirs of silence, which made the tablet like so many of the other tablets of *Gilgamesh*. And her weakness with Assyrian again impressed itself upon her. In a blink, she remembered the mildewed pages of her father's manual in her childish hands, thickly yellow pages that were old even then, aged with the grit of learning, she laying stomach down, her saddle shoes upraised in the air like antennae, teaching herself this language that was supposed to be dead, while her father forever inclined towards his desk, his back as erect as a tombstone, his pipe venting the calm furnace of his mouth.

"Lu?"

Her eyes scanned the claustrophobic geometry of the cuneiform, like a torrent flowing onto the cliff above the Sea of Time. "*Di-ma-a-a*," she read, *yes*, the lines and triangles beginning to pulse in her viscera, her feet pivoting in her boots, she read:

"Tears are the flood of heaven, when not even the light of Shamash himself can crack into the heart of Ishtar, and night itself flees from the shame of her touch, dousing the stars, one by one. Her cheek was—rude—with the blood of her husband. The cornucopia of his manhood rotted in the sky, and melted the horizon. Ishtar stalked bare-footed into the Kingdom of Night. She murmured her disgrace. Not even the wind would send any reply through her bedraggled hair, through the concupiscent hoops of her ears. Not even the midges would touch her skin. Thus she walked for centuries of man's time, a stranger to herself, forgetting the sensation of touch.

"The pride of Gilgamesh wrought such a harvest as this. The flame of Enkidu's friendship scorched love itself. For Ishtar never stopped mourning her loves. She never stopped mourning Tammuz. Not when she furnished Ur with concubines fit for the Palace of Gold. Not when she coupled with the Bull of Heaven. Not when she breathed the shallowest breath. For Ishtar loved Tammuz for all time. And he was a man. A gentler man than Gilgamesh.

"Centuries before the gods had dreamed the greatness of Gilgamesh unto flesh, Tammuz had blessed the earth. Tammuz danced with the nightjars to the music of his trilling reed. Tammuz raced with the Idigna (Tigris) and the Buranun (Euphrates) like over-eager children. The white earth between the waters grew green. Even the palms in the swelling grass danced their dance.

"Ishtar smiled for the first time ever.

"This troubled the gods, who loved Tammuz above all mortals. The precipices of Heaven were Themselves moved by Tammuz's music. Their creation the earth was growing more beautiful than even the gods had anticipated. Watching Tammuz's dance, the tawny sinews of his frolicking arms and legs, Ishtar smiled. The smile of Ishtar, even in half-dream, was like the silver-sheen tongue licking across the tatters of the sky. The balance of Heaven and Earth was already endangered. The gods might have tumbled out of Heaven.

"Ishtar herself left Heaven, as was her habit, to plough darkness into the night on her chariot of lions. To sow the seeds of lust. To make the earth hungry for life. But with Tammuz the earth was becoming ravenous.

"One night, as she rode over the firmament, she felt the pulse of the drum, and the tickling of the air that was the reed of Tammuz. The egrets harmonized from the swaying trees. The crocodiles stood upon their hind legs, whomped their mighty tails, and waved the giant Vs of their heads. Even the camels strutted across the fields.

"Instead of progressing across the sky, Ishtar circled her chariot over Ur, and watched the celebration. The song stretched further and further in time, growing ever faster and faster. The swallows crashed into the date trees. The pounding of the crocodile tails became confused, syncopated. Gazelles collapsed. Tammuz himself, his muscles glistening, ebbed in his piping, as Ishtar's chariot descended to the wheat grass.

"Tammuz dropped his pipe. He had never seen anything so beautiful, even in a world of nothing but beautiful things. He gasped when this divinity knelt down before him to pick up the reed. She smiled at him. And the world cracked.

"Silent footfalls led them inside the tent of Tammuz. The night trailed like smoke from Ishtar's long, dark hair. Tammuz unbuckled her boots, laved her sacred feet. Laughing—yes, laughing—she went inside the lattice layer of his bed, and lay upon her back, her hair flowing over luxuriant cushions. Behind the mesh, Ishtar's eyes glinted like a very rapture of diamonds. Tammuz dropped his sweaty garments onto the tent's ground. He cleansed his own powerful feet in a basin of stars. And he clambered through the delirious curtain, onto the bed.

"As flesh learned flesh, conjoined skins thrilled to soul, bubbling with the genius of divine maidenhood. The wisps of Ishtar's dark mane enwrapped their palpitating nakedness.

"The next morn, Shamash launched his chariot into the sky and was confounded. In the faltering gloom, the Idigna and the Buranun were outspewing their banks. Gazelles sputtered hopelessly through muck. Bevies of ibis fluttered the uncertain sky with their departure. The earth liquefied around the roots of the great unsteady trees. And the night did not surpass Ur at all.

"Angrily, Shamash stabled Ishtar's lions. He surveyed Ur from aloft the Celestial Stables. The tent of Tammuz was an arcade of tingling sighs. As time passed, Ishtar's chariot deteriorated into the white sand, littered with the bleached bones of the dead. The sand slithered. The Idigna and the Buranun parched to a mere gurgling of tar.

"The air rippled—*I cannot guess this gap here*—locusts rasped from within themselves—the eye—a scar blossoming unto—not even the smallest—the finger of a dream—a sea of glass—the lutes of Her eyelashes—the cold tapers leaked—the Drum of Death ripped—the judgment of Crowns gasped—the milk of the stars—so:

"Tammuz was, siphoned, through the sifting sand. Ishtar's bracelets jittered as she lost her hold. The ground repelled her hands. Scarabs shrieked their very blood. Senseless, Ishtar emerged from the flaps of her lover's tent. The orange sky was fretted with vestiges of the night, black constellations hovering over the desert. She was shivering. She was unable to cry.

"She felt, even then, a stirring in her abdomen. Her divinity was with child, with the great bull, when she arrived in the Palace of Dust, to beseech her sister for the return of Tammuz, her lover. Her lover who would never be returned, but would dwell everlastingly in the Forgotten Dungeon of Allatu. The ruined lover Gilgamesh would shame her for. The ruined earth. The night without stars."

Guy's head was tilted. In the lenses of his Wayfarers two little Lulus, her auburn bangs sweeping across her glittering cheekbones, looked rueful in the industrial light of the tablet room. His enormous bulk, in his black tuxedo, was erect, his large fists at his side, clenched, whitening. His inky lips pursed.

Archibald stepped forward, his black tasseled loafers scratching the floor. "What does this story mean?" he asked, rubbing sweat from his curly brown hair.

"It's a tragedy," said Lorrie, the spikes of her hair shadowed longly on the floor.

"It's *our* tragedy now," said Lulu.

"Y[es]," half-whispered Guy, "it certainly is."

Chapter 14:
Shamash's Crack

Everyone was exhausted, but too proud to show it. Considering the many tribulations it took to get the thirteenth tablet, there was no telling how difficult delivering it would be. Lulu lifted it up and squeezed it into a patent leather backpack filled with squeaking Stryrofoam peanuts. She slipped the straps over her leather jacket, and let the weight settle into her shoulders.

Across the pure white room, Reginald opened a red door leading onto the mid-level veranda of the ziggurat. The entourage loped outside. Above, the horizon held its stars. To the right, all that remained of the hanging garden (a matrix of charred, curlicue roots) hissed at the floor. The forest beyond, too, crackled with a pleasant reek of natural ash. Archibald, last among the shuffling entourage, watched the door, which looked like sandstone on the outside, disappear into the steep incline of the wall with a crisp thump of extinguished light.

Simone slouched on the parapet's edge, a flashlight gripped in her hand, the long cylinder's end propped between her bare shoulders and neck, the sharp smear of light aimed upon the text of *Dioramas of the Inquisition*. Sybil slipped off one of her diamond-encrusted pumps, and rubbed the instep of her size-six foot. Trudy yawned, her jaw elongating from the roundness of her cheeks, one arm stretching tall over the concentric bangles of her dress, over the black curls of her short hair, her long fingers darkening the specks of stars.

Reginald wheeled a tremendous brass tureen of Turkish coffee from person to person. To each, a stone cup radiated indigo filigrees into the dimness, an intricate glowing with each ouzo-laced sip. Pasha tilted her mouth back, and drank her cup with one breath. Simone, sipping, scissored her legs as she tried to read. Guy curled his fingers, inward, flexing his fists, and pacing across the stone tiles.

"What t[ime is] it?" he asked. Archibald overturned his wrist, shoved his midnight blue cuff down an inch: 1:34 A.M. Guy heard the tock-ticking of the silver, like the drip, drip, drip of the Muses's milk. Sometimes, Guy thought, the right tune will save your life. Melodic words almost beyond numbering. This great metaphysical miracle of sound. And this night was only more pronounced a night, a night leaking out history, leaking out divinity, and if not his song, then nothing. If not this band, if not *this* night, then all will sift through the inwardness and conjoin with the sands of the void, the void conjoining with the contracting, membranous heart of (of (of))—

"So what now, Guy?" sighed Aleister, leaning against the ziggurat wall.

"We need to get this tablet to [Ish]tar, *tout suite.*"

"How?"

"Forthward."

"Guy," asked Aleister, "which way *is* forthward?"

Guy pursed his glossy black lips into a furtive smile. "Ah: so." And then, craning his neck, the Gaultier gauze bunching up, he asked, "Can y[ou] hear that?"

The guitarist poised his frowsy head into that infernal air, cupped a tattooed hand over the scar leading up to his ear. "You mean that crinkling, from the fires?"

"No."

"Then what? A mosquito?"

"Per[h]aps—a really big one."

"Guy," interrupted Archibald, "perhaps a meeting is in order?"

"Shore. Huddle up, my ponies! And you too, if you please, Reg."

"Very good, sir."

"Reg, is there a [valet] at the house who can—" Guy said, proffering the frayed cuff of his jacket.

"I think we can do something about that, sir, that should be satisfactory," said Reginald, who slipped the long strip of a tape measure from his collar.

"What is that for?" asked Archibald.

"The show."

"Come on, is there going to be a show?"

"There's always go[ing] to be a show, Arch. It's in the contract. Say, what's that?"

A dull whistle marred the ringing silence.

Simone turned a page. Pasha smacked her lips over a long sip of another helping of coffee. Reginald stretched the tape measure across Guy's big back.

"Guy, focus!"

Guy threw off his Wayfarers and blinked his black eyelids, the fading turquoise of his irises swiveling in the whites of his eyes. "Arch," he slurred, "Yoooou [are a] handsome bastard." And then: "Map!"

Lorrie unfurled the huge gray paper with a magician's gesture, the brandishing of a cape. Apart from the grid, the surface looked plain, as if wiped clean, or shaken like an etch-a-sketch.

"You know, the map wasn't all that useful before," interjected Lorrie, "it was that crazy horse who sort of interpreted it."

"That was a whole h[our] ago," said Guy. "This is [now]."

"Now is not exactly now, you know," said Lulu.

"Qu[ite]. Let us *try*."

"If you consult the southwest quadrant of the map—" said Lulu.

"Yes?" asked Guy.

"No, Guy, the *other* southeast quadrant—here!"

Guy clomped onto the twisted corner of the map where Lulu's two fingers pointed. Crude strokes now indicated the "Dreamland Fairgrounds," the Tigris and Euphrates, the ziggurat, and a teeny tiny Guy standing just before Guy's actual wingtips. Guy removed his foot, revealing a very tall doorway before the very small Guy.

"Reginald?"

"Yes, sir?"

"Whoever drew this m[ap] is guilty [of co]pyright infringement."

"Are you certain, sir?"

(The miniature image of Guy blinked, and a ™ materialized over his head, like a halo.)

"More to the point," said Lulu, "it doesn't seem to be yielding up any of its mysteries."

"I must confess, miss, that I am not surprised."

"You've done this before?"

"I am acquainted with this *sort* of thing, if not precisely this thing."

"Do tell," said Guy.

"I'm sorry, sir."

"You're [not] at liberty to—"

"Yes, sir."

"Reginald, so far [this] evening we have been thrust into the Ur of *Gilgamesh* and, ummph, other places. I need you to help [us] back *into* the story."

"So we can destroy it some more?" asked Blee.

"I would pre[fer] the term 'artistic collaboration,' you," said Guy.

"Might I suggest the lower level of the temple, sir?"

"What's down there?"

"I am not certain, sir," said Reginald, "but it is the only place you've not yet been in the temple, and so is the likeliest place from here," pointing with two fingers at the tip of Guy's wingtip, "to there," pointing at the miniature Guy before the big gate on the map.

Lulu quivered, gazing at the map's doorway. "Things have only started to get rough," she said.

"What do you mean?" asked Trudy.

"What *is* that noise?" said Lulu. The whine had become a spattery moaning. A storm of embers burned down from high up in the night sky. Embers that were growing.

"Down, down, down!" growled Guy.

The Posmodernaires fled down the long column of ziggurat stairs, Sybil hopping on one foot to strap her glistening shoe back on. Aleister tripped over her athletic, statuesque ankle, and nosedived thirty feet down atop the crumbling steps, coming to rest on the turret in the middle of the structure. The Postmodernaires hoisted him up and heaved him onto the lower veranda. The other bandmates and Archibald scampered behind them all, Blee giggling for reasons passing all understanding. "[In, in], in!" growled Guy, shoving them into a doorway, counting them mentally ("Sixteen, seventeen, and, yes," he thought, "I am eighteen"). He looked up. Steel geometric atrocities flamed screaming above. Satellites careened. "Reginald?" he called out, but the valet wasn't there. Guy hurled himself into the black rectangle.

Once again, in the dark: Archibald's hands were on the floor, sweat trailing down his forearms and trickling onto his hands. He felt silk bristle against his cheek. A spike heel stabbed his fingers. (He wondered if it was *always* this much effort to put on a show.)

Click. A confusion of flashlight beams, like the dancing spotlights warming up the start of a show, denuded the blackness. Guy moved very, very fast.

"Whatcha looking for?" screamed Aleister, blood smeared across an illuminated cheek.

"What [is] this?" asked Guy.

"A granary, I think," said Archibald, struggling to his feet.

"Smells like grain," said Pasha, swinging the beam of her flashlight around earthenware bins, "is that millet?"

"Not helpful," said Guy in a frenetic blur.

BOOOOOOOOOOOOOM went the ground, with a quivering tectonic echo, in a low, visceral frequency, that shivered, everyone, into a heap.

"What is that?" yelled Archibald.

"We n[eed] more time!" yelled Guy.

BOOoo

Booo

BOOOOoOOOM, ^bounced the ground.

"Gasquigg[a]splorch!"

The entryway imploded with a squinching of incandescent metal, the oversized debris illuminating the large chamber with a hot amber glow. a series of earthenware tubs lined the walls.

"We're trapped!" screamed Trudy, kicking at a reddened solar panel that scorched the sole of her shoe.

"Move, move, mo[ve]!" said Guy, uplifting himself. He ran between the rows of giant silos, towards the far back wall of the ziggurat, the entourage jostling behind him. He pried a hand-plow from the ground and swung its flinty curve against the stone. He sparked the wall.

Archibald pried another loose, and wheeled the tool in the air in between Guy's strokes, until a brilliant light snaggled into the dark, and they swung several more times, chipping away until a white hole bled through.

BOOoBOOom!

"Hurry your [ass]es!" shouted Guy, shoving Pasha's head, and then her posteriors, into the hole while Thor himself was trash-canning the very song of the earth. Guy scanned each body as it hurtled into the gap, and then crammed himself into the light, just before the ceiling of the ziggurat fell.

Chapter 15:
A Straight Line is the
Most Crooked of All

The dunes were brilliant and endless under the low sun, a horizon devoured by a whispering of sand. Mangled steel quivered from the brown swell of ground from which they had just emerged, the hillock melting from seismic erosion. Everyone hastened to a dune above and stood panting in the white light. They seemed to be the last creatures in the world.

"Nice job, guys!" said Guy, who preened sand from the sides of his chalk-stripe jacket, reached inside a pocket, and plucked new Wayfarers out.

"Does he buy them in bulk?" asked Aurora.

"Yes," said Archibald. "Might I have a pair?"

"How did you know to break out," asked Lulu, "into a new dimension?"

"Is this a [new] dimension? When in doubt, I just break something."

"Are we safe?"

"Doubtful."

"Then what do we do?"

"We wait for the madn[ess] to come to us, for a change."

"And how long will that take?"

Guy tilted his head and arched his eyebrows, abdicating all responsibility over the time, and it was only then that Guy truly wondered at *why* this involuted, Alice's-

Adventures-in-Wonderland apocalypse occured in a slithering wrinkle of time, in the Middle East long before it was the middle or east of anywhere, back when it was the *center* of anything and everything worth mentioning, but if that were truly so, then where the Hell were all the people? You might think he lacked a civilized degree of curiosity—to only notice now. What can we say? The Man is an egotist who likes to sing. There he is, sweating (how he hates to sweat!), as he tries his best to look like a statue, a watcher of the desert, while his black eye shadow hardens behind those classic Wayfarers.

A sprocketty drone punctuated the coughing of the winds. Lulu looked up from draining the sand from her boot. A dot on the undulant horizon expanded into focus. The vehicle roved down and up the dunes, and at the crest of these arcs, the band saw, just over the steering wheel, a blue-red smear that focused into the angry baboon nose of its driver. They waited, and when the buggy arrived before them the jinni sprang out without even bothering to put on the brakes.

"What do you people think you're doing?" he gabbled, his elongated snout snapping.

"Not [dy]ing? Say, where the hell did *you* fetch that [bug]gy? We could've used that earlier."

"Shush," commanded the lanky jinni, stalking up towards Guy. "Where is the Fruit of Life?"

"Back there," said Aleister, pointing where the sinkhole had swallowed up the satellite's mangled remains, "and to the left."

"You think this is funny?" said the jinni. "Do *not* think that I can always keep helping you like this."

"My s[im]ian brother, I'll not [dig]nify that rather dubious assertion with comment. As for our probl[em], right now? What [do] we do?"

"You've fetched the tablet on your own."

"Yes. Maybe."

"But getting it to her will be tricky."

"How t[ri]cky?"

"My lord has her, you know."

"No, [I] *don't* know. Where is she?"

"I do want to help you. But you'll need to go back."

"Back to what?" sputtered Guy, swirling his arms 360º.

"No," said the jinni, "back to when. He will never relinquish her now. But if you go back into time—"

"Even [more] back in time?"

The buggy, which had coasted several dunes away, bumped into something invisible.

"Time is of the, ummm, essence," said the jinni. "You must find him when he is—"

"And how do we [find] him at all?"

"Simply do nothing."

"What do [you] mea—"

But Guy was already sinking into the sand, and so was everyone else, sifting through the dust, which was sinking into itself: suffocating them: compressing them in darkness: silting their mouths and nostrils, impressing upon their souls the gravity of gravity, the screams of scarabs, a skeletal salience in that essence issuing inside itself, atavistic echoes of gelatinous t i n t i n n a b u l a t i o n s , t i g h t e r , t e c t o n i c m e l t i n g , *c t h* *t h* *th th*

tho

thon

thonic

thonical,

and around

and   floated

their   bodies   up

and down, \$1.34 million of

couture fluttering in such gravitational

suction, a smearing of coming-going clouds,

stomachs involuting as if seeping five gallons of

mercury, the compasses of their minds jiggling until

the needles snapped into the past of the past, until,

until, until, a twitch of plaster disintegrated around

them and they plunged, arms grappling and legs kicking,

into a deep confusion of lines that slowed down into a

tickling of hay.

"Achoo," said Aurora.

Guy spurted muddy grit from his mouth, and with a deep, guttural inhalation noted the musicians and shards of plaster flopping onto the wheat-stalks around him, which bounced him onto the stony ground.

"[I think I] hurt my hip," moaned Guy, throwing a loose brick from beneath his back. Looking skyward, his vision was hazed, as sand spiraled down from the heavens. This astronomical helix was silky, and reminded him, for all its ease of texture, of trap-angels he had once made at 2 A.M. at Pebble Beach with Harry Connick, Jr. "Aurora [borealis], or St. Elmo's lighter?" Guy asked no one in particular.

"I think it's the middle of an hourglass," said Lorrie Arkitron, "I think it's the middle of an hourglass."

"I dzink wee've become dze hahdest wohking band en dze wohld, euh?" said Philippe, half-gazing at this atmospheric whorl of dust, and giving Guy an arm to heft up with. The umber stain on the lower side of his shirt looked wet. The others crawled out of the hay

"Are you okay, boss?""

"Never ARRR[RRGGGGGGGHH]HHH mind"

The room was half-lit, motes glimmering among the multiple shafts of sunlight coming through the ceiling. Aurora plucked straw from the feathery swells of her red hair. Archibald gave Trudy a pull out of the haystack, their handclasp lingering.

They swept aside a curtain and staggered into a narrow alley, the sky only a long azure vein above concrete walls. A blind potter, seated on the ground, concentrated on the brown clay gyrating on the wheel between his feet. A man in a white linen smock led a donkey past them. The donkey stared with its big, dark eyes.

"Lu," said Guy.

"I know. We are back in—Ur."

"How d[o] you know for sure?"

Lulu hustled up the rungs of a ladder. Balanced near the top, she clutched the building, and gazed around: the rooftops regressed for perhaps a mile, trapezoids piling atop each other with a cubist chaos of precision, Cezanne circa 2700 B.C. She craned her neck, and her green eyes focused. From those white shapes that resembled the jagged floor of a dream city rather than the rooftops of one, a large palace rose into the graying sky, and across that landscape was a ziggurat. On the three long ramps intersecting the structure, dots moved. Dots of people. Lulu crept down the ladder, the heels of her boots cruxing on each rung, until she was low enough to hop down, with satin pleats whooshing over her knees in a flounce of ruined modular swirls.

"That way to the zig," she said, pointing behind them with two fingers, her nails bloody red.

Everyone they met on the street stared away from them, blank swollen eyes scanning the little arabesques of dust. Guy led the entourage through the pathways, with huge steps, and from block to block hastening his pace. Hustling behind him, Lulu saw discolorations on the ground, and when she stooped down they seemed like faint, size-14 bloody footprints. She reached out to grasp the sleeve of his jacket, and then again, but he was always one lurch ahead of her stride. When she lifted her boots into a jog, trying to get to him, he was running, then, his hands straight out, arms pumping.

"Lulu, slow down!" said Simone.

"Stop him!" said Aleister.

Guy slammed against a wall in making a turn, and then bounced right back into a sprint. Lulu felt her ribs ache from running, and the muscles in her feet smarted in her boots. Her sweaty auburn hair drooped, and her torn dress flailed up her thighs.

"Guy, cease!" she yelled.

"Is he possessed?" she thought. "How can he keep this up?" She twisted around to look behind her, and the rest of them were spread out like a race, Sybil tottering as she yanked off her diamond-encrusted pumps.

And then Guy was not in front of her, nor had he turned right, towards the ziggurat. The footprints instead went—

Trudy and Simone bumped her.

"That way!" Trudy said.

There the Man zoomed down a street to the left, *away* from the ziggurat. "What the—" said Lulu, but then dashed after Trudy and Simone. There was a crash behind them. Archibald hurdled Philippe, who had collided into a gourd of wine, and Concetta's blue patent boots clicked *allegro*, the toes scraping the ground. Lulu turned forward and could barely see Guy, his overlarge fists churning.

Lulu remembered, in a single flash, a time when her face was mashing her nose down against a tabletop, her sweaty, auburn hair crawling with sickly airs, in some murmuring necropolis of a bar in the underside of Tangiers. She had traveled to the tip of the African continent to chase down her college boyfriend, who spit in her face in the lobby of the El Minzah Hotel, and, when she tried to hold him, threw her onto the henna-colored tiles. Three hours later she slumped in the darkest brasserie, where she drank two bottles of raki, and tried not to slur her words in rejecting the solicitations of the male patrons. She couldn't understand their words, but their pinched smiles and squints told her enough about what threatened her there. She wanted to leave, but didn't have the strength in her legs, and worried that she might fall asleep and never return home, not that she had a home to go to.

And then this man, straight out of a D.T. hallucination, with darkened eyes and lips, his neck wrapped up, walked over to her, looming, and spoke in English:

"I am all for drinking," he said, "but drinking [a]lone makes me melancholy. Will you join me?"

Lulu thought, since the table was *hers*, that he in fact was joining her, but all her mouth could manage was "yes."

"C[api]tol," he said, and sat across from her, holding some nuclear concoction that illumined his face with a phosphorescent green glow.

"Who are you?" she managed, after two cacophonous songs had come and gone on the p.a.

"Call [me] Guy."

"Guy *what*?"

"Just Guy."

"What—is that thing—your voice keeps doing."

"It's a long story."

"I have forever."

"Can[cer]."

"That wasn't a long story."

"No, I guess not."

"I'm sorry." She reached out a hand to his. It must have been the raki.

"Thank [you]," he said. "And now, why not [tell] me your life [stor]y?"

Lulu convulsed with tears. She told him all about Thomas, how he had been her boyfriend for two years at the University of Chicago, how he had ditched her at graduation, how he claimed to want to travel to discover himself, and revealed how much he loathed her.

"Some people [are] quite empty," Guy said, "and think they can f[ill] that empt[i]ness with the world. All that does is spread the [emp]tiness around."

Lulu stared ahead.

"Thomas doesn't loathe [you]," Guy said. "He loathes his incapacity [to] feel love for one [of] the loveliest nymphs [ev]er deposited on this sphere."

Guy never let go of her hand. She looked at him, but, this gothic weirdo wasn't mocking her. She wiped her cheek, and felt the oiliness of her running mascara, felt the sweat and grime and spittle in her hair, sensed the hardened lavender lipstick upon her lips as she tried not to smile, or grimace.

"Are you making a play on me?"

"No."

"Really?"

"Tell me [the re]st of your story."

And so Lulu told him about her lonely childhood, her mother's deteriorating sanity, her father's monomaniacal absorption into his archeological work, his pathological need to do all in his power to scientifically inhabit a different world than the one he lived in. After he died, she commenced on the path of a party girl, yielding to her Dionysian impulses to dance whenever and wherever the 1990s would let her; but she also yielded to the Apollonian impulse to follow in her father's scholarly footsteps, studying archeology and impressing her professors, even in light of her considerable pedigree. Only Thomas had seemed to understand her need to be both these women, to understand that she was these *two* women, not even her few friends understood—but now she had to face the fact that what seemed like his understanding might have been the blindness of mutual solipsism. He never objected to her conflicted aspirations because he never knew she had any aspirations, and she never knew that he never knew. And here she was, across the globe, a cipher in a ledger that no one would ever read, an empty egg cracking in the back of the fridge.

"Home," said Guy, "is wherever you lay [your] hat."

Lulu held his hand, and looked with anguish into those dark-lidded eyes.

"Mister, what am I going to do?"

"Would you [like] a job?" he said.

"Doing what?"

"Singing. Dancing."

"How do you know I can dance?"

"Your gams tell [me] so."

"How do you know I can sing?"

"I've heard you cry. The [real ques]tion is, do you want the job? [Do] you want the life?"

A black dot heaved, diminished down the graying frankincense-haze. The sticky impressions of size-fourteen soles extended in a line, gory icons on a life-sized treasure map, to orient Lulu. Her toes burned inside those motorcycle boots, sprinting, thick heels never touching down. Sybil whipped past her, those glistering shoes clutched in one wide-swooping hand, the electric blue fabric of her miniskirt flapping, the creamy satin blouse agitated with difficult breathing. Puffs of Chanel no. 12. The sky drizzled sand.

A syncopated clop-clippety-clop resounded in the whorl of Lulu's ear. Something banged into the back of her leather jacket. The beige whir of what appeared to be a dromedary held the bucking form of Archibald, zooming by Sybil. Trudy and Aurora whizzed by her. Lulu shoved off the wall and churned her arms and made her molten legs move. Her auburn hair felt gritty.

She limped and limped. Something clamped her forearm. Philippe. Trotting beside her, lending her a smidgen of his strength. His cigarette pinched between thin lips. His black vinyl jacket crinkling. Faster. Come on come on come the hell on. Oh. There. Up there.

The palace.

Guy and Archibald stood before the tall bronze gates. There was some hullabaloo with the guards. Guy's mottled-blue eyes stared into the dusty sky.

"What's happening?" Lulu managed to say.

"I hope we [have]n't missed it," said Guy, leaking blackly through his midnight blue shirt.

"Missed *what*?" huffed Lulu.

The gates cracked open.

An old man enwrapped in ceremonial robes walked out to them.

Archibald knelt down, the tip of the old man's beard tickling his nose.

"What do you want?" the man asked.

"You are an attendant to his majesty, Lord Gilgamesh?" asked Archibald.

"I serve at his pleasure," said the man. "And you?"

"A priest, I am the servant of his eminence, Sir Guy, he who sits on the royal throne of, ummm, Psychotopia."

The priest squinted at Guy, who eyed those twitterpations in the sky.

"What does he want?" asked the priest.

"Sir Guy wants you to convey a very important message to Lord Gilgamesh," said Archibald, "Immediately."

"His majesty is observing the death rites of his beloved friend, Enkidu. Why should I dare to interrupt them?"

"How long's he been at it?"

"Six days."

"That sounds like a reason."

Lulu thought she saw Guy's lips uplift in the minisculest of smiles.

"He would slay me for such an impertinence. What message do you have the temerity to insult him with?"

"Tell your king the Future [has] arrived," said Guy, "and that the Future has brought a s[ong] to sing—in [hon]or of his dead friend."

Chapter 16:
The Jeweled Worm

The Great Palace was more modest than the ziggurat of the goddess. The taste of darkness: dew and dust and almost-sentient burnt honey. Columns extended, shadows within shadows, darkening each footfall. King Gilgamesh slouched upon his throne. He groped his concentric swirls of beard. His glistening robes reeked.

Or maybe, thought Guy, *the stench is the corpse.*

Across from the throne, twin successions of candlesticks stretched along either side of a bier, ambrosial wax veining down their stems. A plateau of flesh, enwrapped in dark robes twinkling with vapors and jewels, lay between the little lights. A red sash was in his hairy hand. Better, Guy thought, not to breathe. But still he shuffled closer to Enkidu's body.

A flaxen mane parted across Enkidu's large forehead. The smile lines along his mouth were lined with diamonds. A ruby adorned each nostril.

Lulu knelt before the bier, a pale knee jutting from the rags of her once-modular dress.

Guy descended to one bloodied knee.

The remainder of the entourage genuflected, before the shadowy remains of Enkidu.

The king sighed.

Guy gazed at the man on the throne.

"How long have I been dreaming?" asked the king.

"Dreaming of wh[at]?" asked Guy.

"A mountain has been gnawing on time."

"Si[re]," said Guy, pursing his blackened lips, "the dreaming—it's not up yet, and it's eroding. We haven't much time."

"You have a song for me?"

"Indeed."

"To console me?"

"To try, [your] higher-ness."

"What is it called?"

"The Annihilator of my Heart."

"An encomium?"

"A sort of dirge."

The king's head nodded.

Everyone arose. The Postmodernaires hurried into a semicircle. Blee thwacked his palms against his tuxedo trousers in three-quarter time. Guy sang a chant, the Postmodernaires adding descending harmonies that cascaded through his baritone:

You're the annihilator of my heart:
I should've known from the start:
    the blandishments,
        the innocence,
            were all you had to impart.
You're the annihilator of my heart.

You're the annihilator of my heart:
I should've evaded your art:
    All our flutters
        in the gutters
            slashed my psyche apart.
You're the annihilator of my heart.

You're the annihilator of my heart:
A flame igniting the chart:
    the determination
        of infatuation,
           that simply had to depart.
You're the annihilator of my heart!

The king clutched his brow. He asked, "That is the song?"
"Yes."
"That was short."
"Gr[ant]ed. Part of its charm."
"The song was for *me*?"
"M[ore or] less."
"I am not consoled."
"Not even a [li]ttle?"
The king gaped ahead before slicing the air with his royal finger. Great Palace guards approached the entourage with a clattering of manacles, a glinting of blades.

"Y[our] majesticalness," said Guy, planting a hand on the king's shoulder, "whether [or n]ot my ditty has consoled you, y[ou]r kingdom, the future of the *entire* [world ne]eds you. And I must add, *I* n[eed] your leadership."

A cordon of blade-tips pressed the surface of the Gaultier gauze.

"Are you a lunatic?" asked the king.
"Not by clinical definitions."
"What is the matter with your voice?"
Guy fluttered his black eyelids. "It is [mech]anical, sire."
"Are you human?" asked the king.
"Immensely."
The king was very still.
"Why did you sing that song?" he asked, at last.
"It passed the time."
"You diverted me from my grief."
"Y[es]."

"Was that song supposed to be about me—my situation?"

"I thought it applied. What [we] lose—it isn't alway[s] our fault. The meaning of [loss— is] that what we really lose is ourselves."

"A dubious possibility," said Lord Gilgamesh, "which does not alter the fact that my friend is—"

The king's gaze froze on his beloved fellow, whose face glistered with those constellations of jewels in the candlelight. Lord Gilgamesh seemed to lose his train of thought. He kept staring, and staring, and staring.

A ruby sparkled. Its red facets seemed to stir in the dark, some trick of the shimmering candle flames. And then it twisted in Enkidu's nose, and pattered to the tile.

"He breathes!" screamed the king, leaping over to the bier. He held his friend's hand; the red sash slipped to the floor. Then, from the now-open nostril, a pale, segmented cylinder, one inch long, wriggled its way onto Enkidu's lip, raised its head, to behold the new world it had found.

"Oil," demanded the king, and servants splashed Enkidu's robes, his long mane, and his tanned flesh in kerosene. The jewels smeared across his face. The worm shriveled with an ultrasonic shriek. The king grasped a candlestick, and dipped its flame to his friend's body. The flame flowed out into a pyre. Smoke unfurled from the fire. The other candlesticks toppled molten wax onto the tiles. The bottom of the bier fractured, the charring body collapsing onto the support-beams, which themselves became engulfed in flames.

(The smell was terrible, Guy thought, but somehow not as bad as before.)

The *bas-reliefs* of the bier crinkled black in the orange-yellow twitching of the flames, and then cracked, fragmented into the debris and ash in the pile, until the embers seethed through white silt, impotently, amidst the darkened confusion of bone.

Gilgamesh was absorbed awhile with those popping cinders, those bones trying to become fire, but after a time his eyes scanned sidewise, drawn to Guy's presence, and the Great Palace guards who still upheld their sword's tips pressed to the bandage around his throat. The king's hard, grey eyes glowered at Guy's upturned chin. The Great Palace guards' fingers flexed against the hilts, knuckles whitening.

"K[illing u]s wo[n't do] you [an]y good," Guy said.

"How can you be so sure?" the king asked.

"Because [it's n]ot our f[ault] you[r pal is] dead."

"Tell me," said the king, swirls of beard quivering, "who *is* to blame?"

"You are," said Lulu, "And Enkidu himself."

Guy closed one eye.

The guards awaited the command.

Gilgamesh stared at Lulu.

"When you decided," Lulu continued in a softer voice, "that you would humiliate a goddess. That you were entitled to."

A tectonic wheeze escaped from the king.

"O come [on]," said Guy, "*whose* [faul]t is it? He w[as hu]man, you dope, and humans—die. You, [me], everybody."

"*I* am going to die?" asked the king.

"Alas [and cr]ap, yes."

"But I don't want to die."

"[I know]."

"I mean, I *really* don't want to die."

"I kn[ow]."

"I mean, I really, truly, really—"

"Yes, [I] know, G."

("Chief," whispered Lulu, "what are you doing?"

(Guy reached back, set his hand on her stomach. "Think [of] the bo[ok]," he whispered.

("But I thought you didn't remember the story of *Gilgamesh*," she whispered.

("It's [co]ming [ba]ck to me, [kiddo]," he whispered.)

"You cannot go back in time?" the king asked. "You can't make your mountain return time back to me?"

"You gotta go forthw[ard]s to go back," said Guy. "The arrow only goes in one direction. The seasons. The years. The centuries. Time. Civilization. Society. Your life and my life and Frank Sinatra's life. The bad. The good. The ugly. The arts. The fashion. The scene. They all change. All progresses forthward. No one, no king, no goddess, no poet or novelist—nobody can propel these enrgies to regress backwards. If you try to stand still, you are swept away. We cannot fight it. But if you swing into the future as if it is inevitable, you can try to steer the bugger."

"Forthward?" asked the king. "How?"

"You have to go back to the source?" offered Lulu.

"There is someone you must meet. It is the only possibility for satisfaction."

"Who is this personage?" asked the king.

"The oldest man in the world."

"And where shall we find him?"

"Faraway."

"Beyond the Great River?"

"And [beyond] wha[t is] beyo[nd] the great r[i]ver."

Chapter 17: The Ark of the Disco

The mast groaned. The cloaked helmsman eyed the passengers below.

Simone tried to mend Guy's ribs with a fistful of rags. His blue shirt was half unbuttoned. She blotted the rag with sticky blood.

"I'm [o]kay," Guy said, trying to pry the cloth from his side.

"*Tut-hut-hut*," she said. She laid a rag over the spot, and then mummified his lower torso as best she could, tying strips together. "You have a broken rib," she said, "your hip is in bad shape, and probably you have internal bleeding."

"That's what I meant," said Guy, squinting.

Further along deck, Lulu murmured to Gilgamesh.

Trudy tried to distinguish the darkness of the sea from the darkness of the sky. Night had fallen so *fast*.

"Here, Trudy," said Archibald, snugging his Colin McFeeny jacket around her.

"What's this?"

"You're shivering."

"This sign of familiarity, hmmm," said Trudy, preening the wool, leaning back into his arms. People will talk."

"Counting on it," said Archibald, grinning, but scanning the dark.

"Hey. What time is it? Our time?"

"3:15."

"That's all?"

"Yeah."

"Are you scared?"

"No. I'm too tired, you know?"

"Yep."

"I don't think I am afraid of dying, if, say, something overwhelming were to happen, like this ship topples over a giant waterfall or something."

"Don't say that," said Trudy.

"I just—I just don't want to die if I can help it. Or I don't want to figure this madness out, and yet *not* be able to save Guy. Did you get a look at him since the palace? He's bleeding out."

"Simone is taking care of him."

"Still."

"I know."

"How are you?" asked Archibald.

She drooped her head, with all its black ringlets, into Archibald's sandy nape.

Lorrie Arkitron paced the deck. Despite her nerves, she listened to the little slaps of her black canvas sneakers on the polished wood, feeling the pleasant disturbances of gravity, the pulls of that invisible moon, in the alert musculature of her instep.

This made her giddy, in her calm cerebral center, this waking oceanic gravity and darkness. This is what dance *essentially* was—and this is what she most wanted dance to be—not some huggermugger of go-go gyrations, but this alacrity of motion that the viewer can only dream of, that the dreamer must not imagine in any ocular sense, but in the vitality of the flesh, in the neutrons of the toes, radiating to the rest of the body, to the capillaries, to the eyelashes, to the fingernails, this tether to the antigravitational pulse of the spheres that is tapping its foot in everlasting waiting, and Lorrie danced her dance in the dark. Why not, if this eve should have no tomorrow?

Philippe Grandeur smoked another cigarette.

The helmsman turned the wheel 6° to starboard.

Pasha sat with her spine rigid against the gunwale, her hands atop her art deco skirt. Occasionally, the boat would plash down, and the spray would wet the filaments of her long, black hair. She wished she could watch something on television, like that votary earlier this evening. Yes. A divan and a television, just breathing, watching, dry. Something to center her.

Sploosh.

She had never been quite this exhausted before. Five years as a chorus girl with this serendipitous musical outfit. "*Я требую продолжения банкета!*" she had yelled on more than one occasion of Dionysian excess, only to remember that her companions didn't speak Russian, although they always seemed to understand that phrase, at least. Hangovers she had endured, as well as an infinity of rehearsals, a grueling show schedule, and after-parties, but the extravagance seemed to be its own catalyst, remaking the energy it spent.

Sploosh.

The only time she had felt this exhausted, down to her marrow, was a misadventure from her youth, when she and her younger brother, Anton, ran away from their uncle Misha in Nizhniye Serg, which was a zillion miles from mother and father in St. Petersburg. That countryside was like a negative image of this oceanscape: white sky over a white land, with nary a horizon. Even at night.

Sploosh.

Misha discovered them two hours later, shivering in a stiff embrace, on a lane the next town over. After creeping up into the seat of the sleigh next to their uncle, Pasha and Anton bundled themselves in deep wool. Misha didn't get angry on the trip back home, the horses' hooves almost silent, every tree skeletal. Misha gazed over the ears of his horse, while tiny icicles formed in Misha's thick, black beard. The eyes of the children shone like little stars. Once back at his house, Misha tucked the children into bed beneath an ermine comforter that baked them warm. Their uncle was a hunter. And they slept like death.

Aurora squatted atop the prow, her boots dangling over the surf. She held the front spar. One of her heels found its way into the side of the figurehead molded to the front of the boat.

Sploosh!

The water was maybe twenty feet below her, not that she could see it. Her other Mary Jane swung like a pendulum from the rocking of the ship, and it felt so good, this simple thing. She could do this for hours, if only there would be some light. This was an ocean of anti-matter, or some less evolved state of matter, before the stuff of the world *became* itself, a black fuzz, this inky navel of dreaming. Or maybe it was just very, very dark.

But whatever there was to see, Aurora would see it first.

"Hmmm," said Sybil, craning down to un-strap the diamond-encrusted pumps from her ankles. Her epiglottis tightened, and the aftertaste of pheasant mousse tingled the muscles underneath her tongue. She put her blistered bare feet to the deck and tried not to think of the seesawing fulcrum maneuvers of her equilibrium right now, or all that black salty water going sploosh against the bow in a detonation of brine just in front of shadowy Aurora. But how could Sybil *not* think of it, with champagne bubbles resurfacing in her throat? Oh. No. Try, try not to think about it. Dream instead of being safe abed in the Floridita, with—

Sploosh!

Sybil clutched the rail, and stood real still, hoping.

Matta clacked over in those silver go-go boots, with a swooshing of her frilly, diaphanous dress, to gather Sybil's dark hair into her gentle fist. Sybil stooped forward, her eyes closed, hoping, waiting, as Matta caressed the small of her back.

The helmsman turned the wheel 5° to port.

Aleister Wrong sat, legs crossed, before the mizzenmast. The palms of his scarred hands cupped his knees. He tried to meditate, to remove himself from this beating of the darkness, from the risks he knew Guy was taking. He lost Guy once, to that purgatory of the sanitarium. Aleister had been his guitarist from the start, his *riff-man*, Guy called him, these two kids overflowing with Dionysian rage so keen to stomp Apollo's teeth in every night, with more kiddoes in some warehouse one more town towards the horizon, and then back again, and then. This purging of THE SOUND.

When he was sixteen, Aleister's stepfather put him in the hospital with an aluminum baseball bat that broke bones in the boy's forearms. When his mother arrived in the E.R. to beg her son not to tell the doctors what happened, Aleister cackled and cackled. "Let me break your arm, and maybe we'll be even, Mom," he said. "Please," he said, "you *must* love him until he kills you. There is no other definition of love. You are teaching me that." Something about his terrible scorn and ruptured humor told her that she had lost her son. She had lost everything.

A week later, with two casts on his arms, he rode his rickety BMX bike down Las Olas Boulevard, with one arm locked in place by a plaster cast that he had adorned with an anarchy symbol, the AC/DC logo, and a misquotation from Nietzsche. In his backpack were a change of clothes, a toothbrush, a set of strings, and his tablature notebook. His crappy electric guitar with the loose neck and splintering frets hung across his back.

That very night, despite the cast, he got a job washing dishes at a jazz club. And he washed dishes quickly, fiercely. During a break between sets, with the washers full and churning their steam, he wandered into the lounge. Sitting at the end of the bar was a tall young man, in a threadbare funeral suit, with black eye shadow, and black lipstick, on his large, pale face. On the footrest of the stool, a ruined pair of Doc Martens tapped to the beat of the bebop oozing over the sound system. The other patrons left the kid alone. Aleister shivered.

The strange, gothic kid swiveled in his seat, looked at the runaway.

"Can you hear it?" he asked.

"What?" Aleister asked.

"The *need* in the music."

"Oh," said Aleister, listening to the saxophonist growl and honk through a melody, destroying it, as the bass, the drums, the piano, kept him tethered to the song, in some sweaty attempt at transcendence. For a short while, he was absorbed by the music, by the urgency of this desire in the sound, and then he noticed those disconcerting kohl eyes staring at him.

"Yes," he said, "I hear it."

"I thought so."

"What's that you have there?" asked Aleister, looking

at the composition book underneath the kid's large hands.

"The future," said Guy Psycho.

Aleister couldn't play at first, but Guy *chose* him, and wouldn't even wait for the arms to heal: "The beat *is* in there somewhere. Just play fast and it'll show up." They practiced in the garage to Guy's family's house. Aleister slept in a brown sleeping bag on Guy's floor before a wall lined with books. Guy sawed off the casts six weeks later.

Before long, playing every night, every song they wrote, every song they knew, mashing up songs they thought they knew, THE SOUND got *tight*. Even in front of kids who were trying to murder you. Guy sang a few shows with a bleeding, broken nose. He always took the brunt of the rage. Aleister's central nervous system eroded the circuits linking fingers and brain, so that alcohol, exhaustion, or being licked all over had no effect on his playing: sculpted riffs meant to rip your scalp off and leave your cerebellum athrob. And Jesus that madman sang OVER that. WITH that. HARD.

Sploosh.

Then the chanting. Jabbering in tongues. Aleister maybe could have handled scat singing, but Guy uttered things that were *words*—just not words to anything like an already existing language. And he screamed these un-words. Standing stock-still and shrieking passionate folderol into the microphone. For like over ten minutes. The band played on, fast, trying to find the Man's beat. Blee loved thumping his trees to those jams, *manics* he called them, but they creeped Aleister right the Hell out. Maybe there was a psychedelic joy to be found in listening to them, but Aleister loathed those exuberant ex-(plorations/ploitations/plosions) of the Man's psyche. A cover of *Surfin' Bird* would turn into an art rock pig-Latin oratorio that might as well be praising the devil's infinite septic tank or be *Paradise Lost* translated into Urdu or else Ronald Reagan's State of the Union address from 1982 backwards masked. The serpent was devouring its own tail.

Before long, Guy would be incommunicado from the time he awoke until six o'clock at night—to the second. They had to move him into the van with the rest of the equipment. He would sit between amps, those black lips smiling, catatonic.

And then he was gone, for ten years.

Sploosh.

Guy got better, in his own bent way. Of course, Aleister missed the old howling voice. He couldn't quite bring himself to *like* the crooning. The electrical distortions of Guy's voice were the moments Aleister now liked best, the imperfections in the silk that he could trust. But this night was stretching Guy apart.

Alexis, in her truant heart, was wondering—*musing*, in fact—that maybe her days as a Postmodernaire were nearing an end. Not because they all might die out here—the inexorable, black pitch of the sea and sky mattered little to her as she held fast to the mainstay, feeling the torsion lift the thick heel of her shoe off the deck—but because, and this came as something of a shock, she missed Kentucky, she missed and missed Kentucky.

Other places managed to resemble *other* other places well enough, but no place she had ever found the globe over could muster any satisfying similarity to home. On Derby Day, Guy always got her someplace posh to watch the race. He could not have been more accommodating, even though she knew he detested horse racing. She was losing her genteel drawl. She was becoming averse to so much time on a bus, seeing the country stream by her, through glass.

Alexis put her heavy heel to the deck, and then stepped her other heel in front of it, and then moved the other heel back, so the first heel again stepped in front, in this walking in place, this swishing of crinoline, this woman suspended by the rope, in this tension, hovering in black air.

Below decks, Blee poked around for rum. He clicked his flashlight, aiming its giant owl-eye glare towards the floor. In an open berth, the skimming of light revealed Daphne nestled in Concetta's arms, both of them bagging some shallow Zs. Daphne's long legs were folded up, her knees jutting, the green in her argyle hosiery radiating. Daphne's brunette curls swirled against Concetta's dimpled chin. Concetta snored, angelically, her kinked, dirty blonde hair a miracle of science.

Blee jimmied lockers, which tumbled with canned peas and spinach and seasick scorpions. Underneath the crosshatchings of the batten, his elongated fingers plucked at rope-coils, tangles of nets. There was nothing, and more nothing, and even more nothing.

And then he went inside the captain's cabin. On the table was a map, very like the one they had received from Ishtar. Blee noticed a fishing pole. He swiped it on instinct.

He climbed up the hatch, hefted himself up to the bottom of the rigging, and ascended the web of rope. His right hand held onto the pole. The left hand, with those long, long fingers, pulled himself higher. His Vans spread for balance. The entourage's murmurings quieted. The shadows of their existence shrank below him. The air was cool, humid.

At the top, he clutched the pull rope and raised his torso against the big wooden cup. There seemed to be no way to clamber inside with only one hand. He opened his mouth wide. His teeth clamped around the rod. He stretched up until his fingertips felt the ridge of the crow's nest, and then heaved, planting his Vans against the shellacked pine. One leg over, then the other. He took the pole in both hands, and then clutched the padded handle of the rod in his left hand, his fingers spidering over its length. Blee unhooked the catch, brought his arm back, and swung his arm towards the starboard.

Screeeeeeeeeeeeeeeeeeyyyyyyyyyyyyyysshhhhh!

Plash

The helmsman blinked, made a series of unpleasant moist noises with his mouth before spinning the wheel 3° further to port.

The fishing line made a gossamer trail in the darkness.

"Do you think he'll catch anything?" Lulu asked King Gilgamesh.

"I hope not," he said, his beard shuddering its curls, "not in *these* waters."

Zlinchhhhhhhh, went the reel. Blee strained in his perch. The rubber tread of his shoe squealed. He braced himself, his back to the masthead, one foot against the wall of the bucket. The reel whirred, and he pawed at its handle with his right hand until he got a good grip. The torsion was shocking. The pole warped with the line. This bugger was *heavy*.

"Cut that out right now," yelled Simone.

The tendons in his forearm flared, his muscles burned, as he cranked. Each revolution happened with a swoop, and then a pause, and then another desperate swoop. The thing on the other end of the line wasn't fighting, but Blee's shoulders, chest, and arms agonized with its weight. The prey was plucked out of the water. Trudy switched on her flashlight and aimed the shaft of light. A brilliant fission of gaudy luminescence careened in two hundred and twelve directions. There, from the end of the fishing line, bobbing over the batten, was a disco ball.

Chapter 18:
Pirate Battle!

"I think," said Aurora, running a hand through her feathery red hair, "I see another ship out there."

"Where?" said Guy, limping to the front of the ship.

"Port, err, starboard," said Aurora, "over there!"

Guy blinked blackly. "A light over [the]re, please," he said.

Trudy cast the beam across the black waters undulating beneath the black sky.

"I can't see [squat]," said Guy.

"Are you *sure* you saw anything?" asked Simone.

"Don't ask that," Guy said. "If she said she saw it, then she saw it."

"I said I *think* I saw a boat out there."

"Where?" Guy said.

"Still out there," said Aurora, pointing.

"I can't s[ee] squat," said Guy. "Hello!" said Guy to the helmsman. "What the heck [coul]d *be* out [th]ere?"

The helmsman released a toxic succession of loathsome, wet sounds to starboard.

"You don't say," said Guy.

"Can you hear anything out there?" asked Simone.

"What's this b[ast]ard want from me?" asked Guy, staring out to sea.

"Who?" asked Simone.

Guy lurched to starboard, and gripped the rail. "Show your cards," he said to the darkness.

"What's going on?" yawned Concetta, crawling with Daphne from the hatch.

"There," said Aurora.

Trudy's flashlight skipped through the infinite black commas of the waves, and caught sight of a roundness-shape that might have been a vessel.

Pop, went the darkness.

The sea churned.

A hundred yards away, the water exploded.

"What the crap [w]as *that*?"

The helmsman whirred the wheel 135°, to better catch the wind. Everyone aboard flopped onto the deck in a human tangle at Gilgamesh's sandals, as the ark turned through the swelling tide. Blee dangled by his sneaker from the crow's nest. The disco ball banged onto the wood, lolling amidst grappling flesh.

The king marched through the pin-wheeling limbs, and rushed up to the quarterdeck. The helmsman drooled tar, little scorpions wobbling past the king's sandals. The waxy canvas of the helsman's cloak quivered.

"Can we out-speed them?" asked the king.

Pop, went the darkness.

The sea exploded.

Plunk, went the hull.

Guy crawled up the quarterdeck. "Can we get there bef[ore] this bastard blows us up?" he asked the helmsman.

"*Slthsshsslushisslsss—*"

"But I thought you said—" said Guy.

A blinding white spotlight encased them.

Ploom! went the other side of the light.

A dot materialized in the mizzen's canvas.

A high spume of water spiffed off the port side.

Simone yanked a sodden, hyperventilating Aurora back on board. Blee plummeted from the crow's nest into Concetta's arms, plopping themselves onto the deck. Aleister, his feet spread apart, hoisted Vernita up onto her ballet flats. The white light was unbearable.

Guy eyed the hole in the sail. "Dodge [ba]ll, huh?" he muttered.

"Guy?" asked Simone, as he hobbled down to the lower deck.

"Not now," he warbled. The disco ball spun towards him in a thousand ricochets of silver luminosity. "Co[me] to papá," Guy said, halting it with his size 14 wingtip. He wrapped his fingers with his pocket square, then clutched the fishing wire in his hands, and dragged the glittering sphere to the middle of the deck.

"Stay down low, all," Guy bellowed, and then swung the mirror-ball like a leaden lariat, until the impetus of its volition extended its perimeter, until it swooped over the deck, until it looked like a star running laps around a deranged god, until Guy Psycho swung it downward and then, on the upswing, let it go.

The disco ball arose and disappeared into that white light. Offshoots of its dazzle scattered up into the void of sky and into the black water below. It arced into the epic cone of light, and landed somewhere with a deep, nasty squinching of glass.

Darkness smothered the light.

"Atta boy!" said Aleister.

Boom! went the darkness.

An electric belch echoed.

The ark listed, rocked from the splash.

Trudy switched on her flashlight, scanning for their pursuers. A glimpse of gray something caught her attention. It was—it seemed to be—the skull and crossbones of piracy. And above it was another flag, rippling with the swan of Mr. Youngerman's crest.

Boom! went the darkness.

The hull belched below.

The arc listed to starboard.

Trudy's flashlight fell out her hand, overboard.

The ark's pace slackened. Crouching low, the helmsman turned the wheel 15° to port. Gilgamesh dodged a swinging spar of the sail.

Boom! went the darkness.

The water concussed ahead of the boat, on the starboard side.

The sails jolted with breeze.

("They are gone," whispered Gilgamesh.

("Not gone enough," whispered Guy, "if [on]ly we weren't *sinking*, we'd be [so] golden."

("Try not to think about it," whispered Gilgamesh.)

The helmsman pushed his hood back, ran his emaciated fingers through what might have been hair. In the shadows of shadows, the helmsman's smile was inscrutable. Guy couldn't be sure if he was only imagining what he thought he saw, as some sort of after-image after being consumed by so much white light.

His wingtips slipped on the slanting deck. He clutched the grab-rail, and tried to *will* the boat to stay above water, long enough to get Gilgamesh a visitation with the oldest man on Earth. To lift the curse of shame. Guy had to hold on with both hands not to slump into the sea.

Boom! went the darkness.

The hull shattered.

The sea gave a jolt, thumping Aurora overboard.

"Hon!" shouted Guy.

"Ummff," said Aurora.

"Are you okay?"

"I'm burning up."

"What?"

"Oh, it's this cannonball between my legs."

Archibald found a flashlight and shone it down. Akimbo on a beach, Aurora lay panting, her poodle skirt wrapped with kelp, and her red hair glued to her face. The ship's hull collapsed beneath the deck.

"Forthward!" yelled Guy, jumping to Aurora on the sand.

The Postmodernaires dropped onto their sundry heels into the sand in the dark without the slightest disequilibrium, an observation Archibald made as his bobbing flashlight hopped with light. Trudy was just in front of him. Lulu put Gilgamesh's arm around her neck and helped him onward, her motorcycle boots puffing up sand. Archibald cast the light back on deck, to make sure none of the entourage was left behind. The helmsman was there in the light. His pointed, silver teeth glinted. The pupils of his eyes were milky white. The parched, blue tendrils of his fingers waved.

Archibald turned and ran after Trudy, and the rest of the group.

The beach's dunes swelled towards a dark wood. The branches scratched at their elbows, at the hems of dresses. Walking on the path, they had to lift their feet high, to yank their shoes free of the weeds. A klaxon whooped some great noise on the beach.

"Stop!" screamed a megaphone.

"Forthward!" Guy whispered.

Aurora picked her way through the foliage until she came into a little clearing, in the middle of which sat a cottage. Several rectangles cast a sallow glow upon the brush. A festoon of smoke lifted out of the chimney. The yeasty smell of baking bread prickled their nostrils. The surf was still audible, despite the ominous racket made by Mr. Youngerman's schooner. Guy rushed to the door, then smoothed down his lapels, checked his hair for debris. Then he knocked on the door, *tip-tap, tip-tap-tap*, Aurora pressed next to him, with the rest streaming in around them. The door opened.

"What do you want?" asked an old man, with a wild tangle of white beard and hair framing his pale, wrinkled face.

"We've brought some[one] who want[s] to meet you," said Guy.

"What's wrong with your voice?" asked the old man.

"Nothing," coughed Guy.

"Please, sir, won't you let us in?" asked Lulu. "King Gilgamesh has sailed through the Sea of Time to meet you." Gilgamesh grimaced a smile.

The old man's sharp brown eyes scanned them. He eyed Guy's throat gauze. "Come inside," said the oldest man in the world.

They shuffled into the cottage, overcrowding the space so much that the old man had trouble closing the door. The fireplace's heat crept through their legs, toasting their shoes.

"Noble sir," said Lulu, "I would like to introduce you to his majesty, Lord Gilgamesh."

"O great king, the gulls have carried news of you even this far," said the old man. "My name is Utnapishtim."

"Noble Utnapishtim," said Gilgamesh, "news of *your*—longevity is whispered by the gods, and is— audible in my lands."

Utnapishtim nodded.

"My companions here and I—have sojourned against amazing odds to be here, for I—have great need of your wisdom."

Utnapishtim sighed. "Noble king—"

"Noble Utnapishtim," croaked Gilgamesh, "since the death of my beloved friend, Enkidu, I have been beyond consolation. I am come—to you, because you know the secret of—"

Gilgamesh collapsed to the earthen floor. A shard of wood jutted from his robe. A congealing of his blood oozed to the door of the cottage.

"Why didn't he say anything?" asked Trudy.

Chapter 19:
An Un-plotted Island

"This can't—" said Guy.

Simone knelt on the floor, her knees splattering scarlet.

"I mean, the *story*—" Guy added.

Simone parted the bleeding fabric of Gilgamesh's robe, tried to get a good look at the large splinter of his wound.

"Is he—?" asked Guy.

Utnapishtim raised a bushy, white eyebrow.

Simone bowed her head.

The fireplace crackled, logs imploding into ash, with an expulsion of peppery soot.

"No!" yelled Guy. "I mean, the %$@*-ing story was #@Ω^@-ing right *there*."

Outside the little cottage, underbrush rustled.

"Lulu?" asked Guy. "Whatever do—"

"I've got nothing," Lulu said. "I don't know."

Several men yelled at one another outside.

"Agéd m[an]," asked Guy. "What [should] we do?"

"What did the king want to ask of me?".

"The [sec]ret of eternal life, which has helped you endure the millennia."

"And what do *you* want to ask me?" asked Utnapishtim.

"The same [th]ing?"

"No."

"How do we [finish] the story?"

"Ah."

Outside: boughs breaking. Chainsaws.

"Please, we're in [a] hurry."

Lulu rubbed Guy's broad shoulder.

"Well," said Utnapishtim, "it seems to me that in circumstances such as this—"

"Yes?" asked Guy.

"You need to go forthward."

"Look here—" Guy said, raising a finger to make a point.

Through an un-shuttered window, a pigeon glided into the cottage and landed upon the chalk-striped sleeve of Guy's arm. The bird lifted its leg, to which a tiny scroll was fastened. Guy tore the tiny rolled paper from its twine, and then with one hand unfurled the text. There, in the center of its surface, was a pure black dot.

The pigeon winked at him, and fluttered out of the window.

"You better find out what he wants," said Utnapishtim.

Chapter 20:
Guy's Dilemma

Guy opened the door and limped out to the little clearing. Mr. Youngerman was there, alone, in his belted gray flannel suit. The older man smiled, tilting his cigarette holder up, smoke wafting between his teeth, out of the sneer of his lock-jawed mouth.

"You're a very difficult man to follow, Mr. Psycho."

"And your g[i]g is out o[f] this world, T.C.E."

"When I hired you, I had no idea how much you and your group would improvise."

"The no liquor [rule]? *That* wasn't in the contract."

"Not my doing, I assure you."

"He's dead, y[ou] know—Gilgamesh."

"Alas, yes. Couldn't be helped."

"I d[on't] believe you."

"I know. Your faith in me is of little consequence."

"How do you figure that?"

"Look—"

"And your lack [of] faith in me?"

"Hmmm?"

"The black spot?"

"Don't take it so literally, Mr. Psycho. I needed to get your attention."

"Now that you have it, what do you [wa]nt to tell me?"

"He didn't like your song, did he?"

"Well, under the [cir]cumstances, it's ra[ther] difficult to—no."

"If I'm not mistaken, you have just about time for one more song."

"And if you *are* mistaken?"

"Then we're all dead, of course."

"You [plann]ed all this."

"No—not *all*."

"Mm-hmm."

"I did the best I could."

"So did I."

"Of course you did."

"So what h[appe]ns now?"

"Try it one more time."

"A song?"

"Sure. A song."

"Not for the old man?" asked Guy, aiming a thumb at the cottage.

"No."

"But all the [oth]er players in this Sumerian drama are *dead*."

"Yes. And they're all waiting for you."

"Waiting for me? Ah: so. Not in your ballroom, [I pre]sume."

"No."

"Didn't think so," said Guy, clutching the wet side of his jacket.

The sky was silting rivulets of dust.

Guy blinked longly three times, making his eyes disappear in the dark.

His synthetic vocalizer inflected each of his breaths.

"Okay, I'll [go]," he said to Mr. Youngerman, "But [please] do me a favor."

"Indeed?"

"Hustle my [peop]le outta here."

"Ah, yes," said Mr. Youngerman, slipping a phone from his gray flannel pocket. "We had anticipated that."

"*We?* Hey, is that doodad going to work?"

"Reginald," said Mr. Youngerman into the cell, "send them forth, please."

A *basso profundo* susurrus emerged from the night.

Pssshhhhh gasped the sound, and then the strain of a simultaneous chugging and pinging döpplered its way towards the clearing.

A silvery yellow glow scraped the brush, fragmenting the darkness with its electric luminescence, until an immense rectangle of chrome burst through a gap in the wild briars.

The door of the bus infolded, and Joseph Boovley stepped down onto the ground. Wog and Wonk clambered huge and quick behind him and advanced between Guy and Mr. Youngerman in a cordon of baleful muscularity. The bodyguards' dark fierce eyes met Guy's, as they crossed the flexing, meaty pistons of their arms.

"How [are] ya, boys," Guy said, sliding an arm over each of their sweeping bulk of their shoulders and slouching in a way that his own largeness became small.

The pursing of their taut mouths signaled the deep shame they felt at being absent while Guy had been putting himself at risk. They were unaccustomed to seeing him injured, or even tired. The pushed-out frowns were all they would do to articulate these feelings (since they *still* had a job to do, that they *wanted* to do, if Guy would give them a knowing nod—they would do something vicious and inexorable right then and there).

Wog and Wonk shifted to gaze upon the aristocratic culprit of this misadventurous evening. Mr. Youngerman smiled. Someone cleared his throat.

"I told [you] that you could fix it," Guy said to Boovely, extending a hand.

"Yeah," said Joseph, gripping Guy's palm, the miniature siren goddess over his metacarpals disappearing under Guy's thumb. "Now are we going to get to Chicago on time?"

"But of co[urse]," Guy said. "Why not?"

The cottage door opened behind them. Simone stuck her head out, her blonde mane swaying, then she stalked out. The rest of the entourage poured out behind her. The oldest man in the world watched them go.

"What do you want us to do, chief?" asked Wog, cocking his sinewy neck towards Mr. Youngerman.

"Yeah, Guy, what's the imperative verb here?" asked Wonk.

"You can leave the old man [al]one," said Guy.

"Okay, boss," said Wog and Wonk in monotonous tandem. But they kept staring, with their mouths pursed, the breath waiting for swift action. Mr. Youngerman smiled again, little billows of smog puffing from his teeth.

"Gents," Guy said, "just make sure that [once] the bus is loa[ded], no one gets off."

"Affirmative," said Wog and Wonk.

"Especially Lu," whispered Guy.

"Yes," said Wog and Wonk.

"Ahem," said Joseph Boovely, "Everyone! If I could have your attention, please. If you are going to Chicago, please get onto the bus this instant."

The Postmodernaires and the musicians of the Guy Psycho band marched towards the bus door, each pace in synchronous movement. Each of them ascended into the bus. Lulu was the last of them, and she lingered, tugging Guy's chalk-striped lapel.

"What's going on?" she asked.

"We've [gone th]rough all the stations of this [Epic Th]ing—reliving it—de-living it, maybe."

"I never quite believed we were *really* doing it all."

"It's been quite a ride, kiddo. [Ev]en for us. I just [hav]e one more thing to do."

"Is it okay?"

"It will be."

"No."

"I have a date [with] a goddess, [to] finish the tablet. Sing [one] last song: a cappella: solo. Me."

"Make it a duet," said Lulu, pulling the hem of modular swirls in her torn dress.

"No."

"Maybe I could help."

"I can't do what I *must* do—if I know that you'll be watching. If you are there."

"You're getting self-conscious on me?"

"In this world, anything is possible."

Lulu smirked, with tears on her glittery cheekbones.

"Tsk-tsk," said Guy, rubbing her auburn hair. "We'll always have Tangiers."

Lulu leaned forward, and kissed Guy's black lips. She gazed at him awhile through her bangs. She rested her head upon his chest. He held her a moment, and then stripped the patent leather pack off of her.

One of her hands held onto a strap, as she gazed at his eyes.

"You're getting on that bus where you belong," said Guy. He goosed her, making her let go of the pack. He twirled her around, and shoved her upward into the doorway of the bus. Her motorcycle boots clomped up the steel steps.

"All aboard," said Joseph, hopping up after her.

"Will you b[e nee]ding a ride, T. C. E.?"

"No, Mr. Psycho, I'm all taken care of here."

"I bet," said Guy. "Okay, my Ws, get [your]selves in there. Mind both doors, and keep *them* closed."

Wog squeezed his arms together and pressed himself through the doorway. Wonk stood stock still, his bald head a second moon on that beach. His lips twitched. "Are you going to be all right?" he asked.

"I think so. *This* time, I almost know [wh]at I am doing. [Get] outta here."

Wonk reached forward, to shake Guy's hand like an industrial vise. And then the bodyguard crossed his arms, stepped onto the bus, the doors sealing behind him. Lulu stared down at Guy, until Wonk yanked her away by the hand, deeper into the back of the bus.

The chrome lurched backwards through the brush with a mighty screeching through branches. The light swooped across the clearing, and was gone. Just Guy and Mr. Youngerman.

"You're good," said Mr. Youngerman.

"Let's just hope I [am go]od *enough*," said Guy.

"Yes, let's," said Mr. Youngerman. "You won't be able to carry that with you, Mr. Psycho," Mr. Youngerman added, pointing to the backpack holding the thirteenth tablet.

"Whyever is [that]?" asked Guy.

"Because where you are going, you have to bring *only* yourself," said Mr. Youngerman.

"Is th[at a] riddle?"

"Not in the slightest, Mr. Psycho. You'll see."

"So I suppose you don't want this tablet for your own collection in Tennessee?"

"We are participating in *living* history, which is a far superior thing to possessing things, no matter how ancient. Haven't you learned that by now?"

"Then what [happ]ens with the tablet, then?"

A great blue heron swooped down upon the clearing, stalking on its spindly legs. With its right eye, the great bird looked at Mr. Youngerman, and then at Guy, before nodding in recognition.

"You've got to [be] kidding," said Guy.

"She can fly with this, and bring the tablet where it must go. I assure you, it will work."

"Really?"

"Really."

Guy outstretched his arm, dangling the patent leather

bag. The tall bird walked to him, opened the scissor of his beak, and clamped down upon the strap. Then it stalked a few paces away, popped up into the air, and with a flapping of its arched wings, alighted into the dark sky.

"I hope [you] know what you are doing, T.C.E."

"How many deaths do you think you have in you," Mr. Youngerman asked.

"I really don't know," said Guy. "But we are about [to find out.]"

Chapter 21:
Seven Thresholds to Death

"Young man," said Utnaptisham, "you'd better hasten. Not much sand left in the sky."

Guy ruminated the warped firmament, rippling smears of black on black. Not even a cricket chirping.

"Yeah, sure" said Guy. "T.C.E.?"

"Mmm?"

"Which [is] the way?"

Through there, and then left."

Guy stumped along, over the bus's tread-marks, through the opening in the skeletal brush. He came to a two-lane blacktop stretching in both directions. He swiveled to the left.

He stood in vast darkness. Blood seeped through Simone's bandages, his tailored shirt, and crawled down the laces of his shoes. He blinked, dark and heavy-lidded, a long time. *Squinted.* The road was a shadow among shadows.

He felt very, very tired. So tired. More tired than it was possible to feel. His eyes were burned-out fuses. The thick darkness was beautiful.

"Forthward," Guy whispered, to himself.

His legs were stiff, these compressions of meat. Each shoe pincered like a vise. But he moved: the shiny leather of each wingtip squeaking with each forced step. *Long strides*, he thought, *favor my toes, heels off the ground.*

He tried to take deep breaths, but the wound in his abdomen clenched into his lungs. His vocalizer emitted vapory sounds.

After a while, the road that had seemed infinite now rose and fell into the middle distance of an abyss. The pain stopped being localized, and instead numbed to a tangy sensation at the back of his brain. His dark, sweaty eyes went bleary, then sparkled. Over the next knoll, he thought he saw a long metallic grate spanning the whole horizon: a belt across the earth. With each pace, the steel arose taller, and taller still, until it looked like a dam for the stars, stored in the back of some celestial funhouse. *One two, one two*, thought Guy, *I'm slouching towards, slouching towards*, but as he lurched forthward he couldn't recall the old poem.

The road rose and fell, and swerved right and left, like a ribbon some god had flopped on a floor. Despite the totality of exhaustion, Guy remembered something he learned two decades ago, reading in the shade of a pine tree: Zeno's paradox, which describes how an arrow reaching its target is a metaphysical impossibility.

All space and matter is infinitely divisible.

The last few inches are not inches at all.

He peered up at the empty sky, which bounced with each footfall. He looked ahead to the colossal grate. He looked down at his swollen, churning feet.

I wonder, thought Guy, *if a little nap here beside the road would do much harm?*

His right thigh quivered, then cramped. He sped up, his right leg rigid and vaulting a little with every other step. *Hep, hep*, he thought. *I don't know what I've been told.*

A tug at his foot. The shoelace of his left foot was untied, two strips wriggling along. Guy knew that if he collapsed, he might need more time than he had to right himself, if he didn't lose consciousness first, if the world didn't end before that happened. A martini—if he got through this, he would treat himself to a martini, the icy fire for himself.

Though I walk through the shadow of the shadow of the valley of the shadow, Guy thought, *I shall fear no draught.*

The gate grew before him, this curve of steel lines across the world. The ground and the sky were blackening, with just this promise of tangible dimension. His soul was a stork fluttering across his frontal lobes. He inched closer to the gleaming barrier.

"Let's [go], Psych-o, [let]'s go!" Guy cheered into the nightless night, his huge mouth agape and cackling.

He looked up. The sheer, metallic plane elongated upwards, almost high enough to reach forever. Guy saw two tiny figures in shiny jumpsuits patrolling in front of the wall, which meant either he was getting closer, or else the nightmare was at least being a very focused one. His leg stopped cramping—or rather, it stopped feeling like a leg, with the purpose of being a leg, and was instead reduced to being a conspiracy of atoms, of molecules, coupling in a kinetic pattern confused with leg-ness.

Not unlike the sensation of being drunk. Guy's gait gained the sort of grace the great misadventures of the evening had made impossible for the last few hours. His skin felt cool, effervescent. Yes, indeed. His bespoke wingtips felt crisp, adhering to the curvature of his oversized feet. He swung his arms wide, not heeding his broken ribs, which, too, seemed to be a memory now, the blood of his blood benumbed. His fingertips felt orange.

The sentries ahead were become human sized now, each step revealing the swollen, veiny musculature of their steroidal physiques pressing against the satiny silver of their garments. He heard the literal *clomp* of their military boots. *Wog and Wonk would have their mitts full with these Bubbas*, thought Guy. *But no matter.*

I am an arrow.
Here is my target.
And the target will know what to do.

(I hope.)

The guards stood at attention, parallel to one another, when he strutted up to the gargantuan barrier.

"Top of the evening, gents," said Guy, beaming a gloopy, black smile.

"Hiya," said guard number one.

"So what's the score? I need to pass through here, *tout suite.*"

"You must gives us something."

"A bribe?" Guy asked. "Alas and crap, my manager has my check—"

"Not a bribe. Like a toll, more."

"Even so, I don't have much to trade."

"Your jacket'd do."

"This jacket?" Guy examined the woolen chalk-stripes, bespattered with at least three types of blood. It still looked fabulous. He sucked in his cheeks,. "This was my first [be]spoke suit. The lapels are divine. The cut— well, no [one else] would look half so good [in] it. I can recomm[end my tail]or."

"Rules is rules, sir. It ain't me or him whose gets to wear it, anyhow."

"Oh, I don't care about that," Guy said. "All right."

He peeled the jacket off and tossed it to Guard Number 2. It looked like a tissue in his massive hand.

A line broke up the steel rungs of the wall, and two rectangles parted from it, doors opening with a hollow, whirring clank. The guards pointed inside. "In with you," said Guard Number 1.

"Thank you large," said Guy.

"Sir?" said Guard Number 1.

"Hmmm?" asked Guy.

"I just wants to say I love your tunes."

"Thank you," said the Man. "Call me Guy."

"I hopes you makes it."

"Me, too."

A stairway had been gouged into the void. Gravity thickened. His eyes strained to imagine outlines, but the steps seemed to catch his feet. He padded down now, the catch in his hip molten and warm and almost pleasant.

Below him, a rim of electric cross-hatchings licked out of the nothingness: a chain-link checkpoint, Guy suspected. A few incalculable minutes later, he was confirmed in that suspicion. A platoon of men in purple camouflage swarmed behind the towering matrix of Xs, like feral cats in a cage, hungry. With shiny rifles, they shot light into the black sky. "Come on!" they screamed.

"What do I do?" asked Guy.

"Give us something!" they screamed. "Hurry!"

"Hmmm," said Guy, musing at the rusty mailbox on a post before the fence. He slipped the heel of his loose wingtip beneath the toes of his right foot and pried the shoe off. The left shoe gleamed in the dark, its taut laces not relinquishing his swollen, size 14 foot. Against a boulder, Guy slouched, trying not to breathe or overstretch or otherwise further abuse his abdomen, as he reached for the laces, and plucked the knot loose, and pulled the shoe from his sticky socks. While the soldiers growled behind the fence, Guy limped to the mailbox, opened its door, and crammed his bespoke wingtips inside. He forced the door closed, and then upraised the mailbox's outgoing flag.

A ratcheting sounded along the perimeter, and a segment of the barrier rolled back, allowing the plum-colored platoon to flow out in their frenzy, their silvery guns agleam, to escape whatever doom that their esoteric weaponry couldn't liquidate behind that fence. When their clomping boots got out of the way, Guy passed through the threshold, his socks on the dusky earth.

The path zigzagged, until the ground gave way to a brick street, and the ramparts of a citadel glistened ahead. Guy managed to run, his brain gelatinous, his flesh both dense and ethereal. The ramparts climbed up the sky. On the side of the street, built into the fortification next to a gate, was a wicket-door. Guy knocked three times. The window swung open. A guard's gaunt face gloomed at Guy from beneath a helmet that appeared to be the oversized skull of some humanoid creature.

"Your fee, sir?" croaked the guard, who stroked his mossy beard, then held out his cadaverous, serpentine hand.

Guy flopped upon the bricks and one by one yanked his thick black socks off. He draped them up into the guard's hand.

The portcullis lifted.

Inside, mosaics glistened in trillions of shades of brown. Guy traced a fingertip along the embedded shards, as if to feel the narratives he didn't have time to study. The murals spanned the walls, the ceiling, and even the floor, in this kinetic frozen-ness. The mosaics beneath him chilled his toes. Guy saw so much, even though there was no clear light source entering this chamber. But his depth perception was compromised, and he couldn't tell how large the corridor was.

Above him, the spastic trajectories of a few bats careened.

I wonder, Guy thought, *if any of these images finish off my story?*

His reverie was interrupted by a cobalt suit of armor, and a threatening spear held by the armor's inhabitant. The visor looked like a long beak.

"Halt," said the knight in a tinny voice.

"Halted," agreed Guy, nudging the spear's point out of his abdomen.

"You must bequeath me a toll for passage forth, sir."

"Criminey," he groused, "Worse than Connecticut."

"I am just performing that which is my duty, sir."

Guy blinked at the knight, whose gaze was a mere long black slit across blue-black metal. Guy contemplated his stained shirt, his chalk-striped trousers, the cuffs slack against his pale ankles.

Guy un-strapped his braces, and unbuttoned and unzipped his pants, allowing the gray wool to droop past his Glenn-plaid boxers down to his feet. He plucked his pants from the mosaic and slung them over the rod of the knight's spear, so that they slipped with heartbreaking obscenity atop the knight's glistening gauntlets.

"Quick," said the knight, with an awkward flourish of his weapon towards the doorway, "I beseech you."

The next passage was filled with mirrors attached to the walls in a variety of frames, duplicating a thousand Guys in all his pathetic absurdity: hurrying forth in his boxers, his shirt, and his wounds. He wasn't sure, but he thought the mirror-frames might be twitching. He coughed, then coughed again, the air gritty, a legion of intruders upon his lungs. His blackened eyes were gooey with liquefying eye shadow. Someone may have been laughing at the sound of crashing glass. It might have been Guy. He was on his knees.

He crawled a long time, blind, scraping the cosmetics from his eyelids, black circles blotching around the sockets.

"Sir?" a woman's voice asked.

Guy arose on his feet.

"Try this, sir," said the voice, and a cream-laden washcloth came into his hand. He rubbed the make-up clear with gusto. A dry washcloth finished the job. He saw a woman in a navy-blue uniform. Her felt pillbox hat clamped down over a chestnut bun of silken hair. Both her cheekbones and chin were dimpled. She took both washcloths from Guy's oversized hands, with no hint of embarrassment or condescension. They stood in a glass room. He leaned on a transparent basin. Eight red laser beams pierced the glass walls at the end of the room, where a gray room beckoned.

Guy's hands shook. The whole world was shaking. There were angels in his eyes.

"I hate to ask, sir," said the woman.

Guy winced a little smile. He unfastened the ivory buttons of his royal blue shirt, and with a wrench of coagulated blood and Simone's bandage-strips, separated the shirt from his torso. He held the garment out to the intergalactic stewardess. The beautiful, uniformed woman folded his shirt with a smile. The lasers disappeared.

"This way," she said, clacking on navy blue heels through the passage. "I can accompany you to the next part, if you like."

"Indeed," Guy coughed. The gray stone walls sparkled, or was it the air? He followed the woman, trying to walk tall, although his feet were slippery, tingling. What he wouldn't give to be a single chestnut filament in her hair, coiled with the others, this line so near, and so irrelevant to, that brain. He wondered what it would be like to be the *particular* absence of the dimples of her chin, or her cheekbones. But maybe, in fact, it felt how he felt right now.

"He's here," she said to someone ahead. The stone room ended in a plexiglass chamber beside a big orange door. The woman pushed his shirt through a hole in bullet-proof plexiglas. From behind a desk on the other side of the partition, an albino man, eyes swollen, breathing through a mask, took the shirt, placed it in a plastic bag, which he then placed in an envelope, labeled *Guy Psycho and the Ziggurat of Shame.*

"You'll need to, once again," she said, "you know—"

"Of course."

"Good luck, Mr. Psycho," she said, clacking away, "Me and the other officers are rooting for you."

"What's your name?" Guy asked, as her footfalls went back, back, back to the room of glass.

"Okay: forthward, then," Guy said.

He bent, weak, to ease the elastic of his bloody boxers down. They clumped down his legs, and he stepped out of them. The pure air tingled his exposed crotch. He felt (almost) free. He leaned his bulk down, in the fullness of all excruciation, to pick up the Glenn-plaid shorts, and force them through the opening in the plexiglass to the attendant.

"My apologies," Guy managed, "for the lack of hygienics." The attendant made a slight shrug.

A buzzer opened the orange door. Guy nakedly limped into a courtyard. Towers were gloomy silhouettes. He heard murmuring from the other side of the yard, a confusion of voices, muted and echoing. He strained to listen, scanning the air for Ishtar's voice, that inhuman sweetness of tone, but the sound seemed too muddy for him to even guess. He strode across the paved ground, each step weighted by the vacant stars, his feet like balloons of milk, harps aflame and pricking into eternity.

Reginald the butler, impassive, in his perfect tail-coat, stood with divine posture, by the seventh door.

Ever so slowly, Guy unwound the whitest Gaultier gauze from his neck, handed it over, and walked through the final threshold.

Chapter 22:
In the Palace of Dust

Dynamos of incandescent dust-motes, cascading.

His pupils contracted: and contracted: and contracted—pinpricks.

Never had Guy wanted sunglasses more. The light! Even when he closed his eyes. His huge hands palming his face.

No proper footing, bare feet shlurping in ether. Don't look down. Yikes. Nevermind.

It's thirteen o'clock, thought Guy. Time to get this show on the road. He had to concentrate on not allowing his atoms to dissolve, these quarter-notes of existence. The hungry powder of the afterlife clung to his translucent flesh. Through a pink gap between his overlapping fingers he discerned breathing walls, a carbonated atmosphere. He shoved his foot forthward, angry, stomping out of the dust-cloud, and then with the other tremendous, bloody foot stomping out of the next dust-cloud. Incense of myrrh wafted. Guy's lungs and gums gritted with particles. Streaks of light and sound. He reached out his hands, wading through these agitations of matter.

Swirls of swirls teetered in place, in a concentric disarray. He stumped between these formations, his pupils quivering between the black slits of his eyelids. His breath felt thick with stale mist.

He passed a royal banquet table, where Julius Caesar blew upon a spoonful of clam chowder, Charles the Sixth sucked his dentures, and Queen Victoria, puffy cheeked, stooped over to extinguish the candles of an enormous pink cake.

Concentrate, Guy thought to himself. *Get to the gig.*

The swirls slowed their gyrations, slowed to an infinitesimal slowness, as he walked along, slowing into a series of kinetic columns that upheld a ceiling of scattering stardust.

I've got sand up my crack, thought Guy to himself. *Get to the gig and let's take a shower.*

The floor twitched, gaseous soot creeping at his feet. Guy stopped. He gazed at a cluster of eddying shadows, at the darkness curlicueing upwards, up a pair of legs, swooping across feminine buttocks, gathered up like long, black hair in a woman's divinely sculptured arms. A woman was turning. A woman turned. A weary smirk crept up her perfect cheekbones. Ishtar.

Guy smiled.

Above them, slumped on a towering throne of marble, the Lord of the Underworld, tracing his own divinely sculptured abdominal muscles, gazed down, yawning. Enkidu knelt by his side.

In a crowded gallery besides Guy and the goddess, the jinni, Mr. Youngerman, and Lillith stood. A great blue heron swooped through a window, glided around the dusty space, and landed, dropping the patent leather backpack. With its beak, the bird unlatched the flap and snaked its neck inside, and wiggled the stone out of it. The thirteenth tablet was at their feet, atop a layer of Styrofoam peanuts in the dust.

"You have a song?" asked Enkidu.

Guy nodded.

"Go ahead."

"Chthngthhk. Mngrmphklp. Mscrntrthnnfrssh." Guy's fingers went up. His throat a maze of electrodes and gears and sludge.

Ishtar's hand touched his back. "Don't try to sing with your mouth," she said. "Sing it with your heart."

Guy believed this advice was metaphysical nonsense— how could he go about making his heart sing? What, pray tell, is the first step in doing that? Of course, Guy could not even ask that question here, unless he could ask it with his heart, and if he could do that, he wouldn't need the advice in the first place. He wondered if maybe the advice was to *think* the song? Or was the point to sing the song to some cardiovascular rhythm? Guy wasn't feeling too well, all things considered, so he doubted the possible wisdom of singing to the rhythm of *his* heart, at this moment in not-Time. He closed the slits of his gray eyelids. Sing the song. He saw no alternative but to try. *A cappella*, from his palpitating heart:

> For all the years I was the man you dreamed of
> You bit your lip rather than reveal your smiles,
> For all the years I was the man you dreamed of
> You escaped like a ghost down all those aisles,
>   When I finally exclaimed your name
>   Nothing would ever be the same,
> For all we had left was just breaking love.
>
> For all the idylls we were dreaming of,
> I walked a thousand-thousand miles,
> For all the idylls we were dreaming of,
> We showed the world a hundred-hundred denials,
>   We never got to lay in the bed that we made,
>   And my debt to you will never be paid
> For all the while we were just breaking love.

For all the years my heart waited for a heart,
All I wanted was for the blessing of a start;
　　But my promises shattered like shame,
　　My empty soul is surely to blame.
For all I had left was just breaking love.

Don't leave, you said, stay right here,
'though you fill my heart with such fear,
You said you'd always stay,
We would find another way
　　　　　for breaking love.

Don't go, you said, stay right here,
'though you fill my heart with such fear,
You said you'd always stay,
We would find another way
　　　for breaking love.

Ishtar reached out her hand, which slipped inside Guy's.

The Lord of the Underworld scratched his scalp, unsettling his horned crown. "Hmmm," he said. "That was—"

"Y[es]?" Guy wheezed.

"—not altogether bad."

The dust whispered brightly.

Enkidu descended the dais, his sandals billowing with each step. He kneeled before Guy. "Have you beheld my friend, King Gilgamesh?" Enkidu asked.

"In[deed, I h]ave."

"How—how is he?"

"He misses [you]. His entire l[ife an epic, to tr]y to fill up how very much he misses you."

Enkidu clutched his face, his mossy beard fomenting curlicues of ash. His fingers flexed. "Lady," said Enkidu, "I wronged you. Such mockery as mine was unjust. There's—"

"I know," she said.

"This part of you, always, here."

"Yes."

"Forever."

"Yes."

"Forgive me!"

Ishtar wept a dark oval, which silted down her perfect cheekbone, and sank into the particulate ground, radiating specks of refulgence. "It isn't your fault," she said.

"Forgive me," said Enkidu.

Her right hand lifted to her face, scraped her cheek. She squeezed Guy's hand hard.

"You—I forgive you," she said.

Guy smiled a big, black smile.

"Now you know," she said to Enkidu, "what it's like."

"I'm so sorry," he said. "I'm so, so sorry."

"I know."

"Do you miss him?"

"Always. Always."

Enkidu arose, strode towards them. He clasped forearms with Guy. "Thank you, whoever you are."

"Me," said Guy. "I'm no one."

The great blue heron flapped cloudily between them, zigzagged hither and thither, squawking through an airy tangle of curtains in the side of the chamber.

"You are an envoy between the worlds," Enkidu said.

"Aren't we all?"

"Some more than others," said Enkidu, ascending the dusty marble steps back towards the tall throne.

The Lord of the Underworld coughed.

"Most dread sovereign," said Guy.

"Don't address his majesty, without being first addressed yourself," said Enkidu, wincing.

"Envoy," said the Lord of the Underworld.

"Sire."

"What are you still doing here?"

"Am I free to, umm, be dismissed or something, your Underworldliness?"

"You'd better. You are boring me."

"And tomorrow?"

"Will be another day."

"Is *she* free to go?" Guy asked, and he felt a tug at his hand.

The Lord of the Underworld, kicking up a golden boot over the side of his throne, squinted at a gnat in the middle distance.

"Yes."

Solid. The dust alive. Ishtar laughing into his arms. A confusion of feet. She towed his arm to the curtains. Skipping. They crept through the damask fabric, a letter leaving an envelope.

The floor gleamed for miles. At the end of the hallway, a red EXIT sign beckoned.

Guy stepped forthward, but found himself tethered by a lovely arm.

"Don't leave," said Ishtar, smirking across her perfect cheekbones. "Stay right here."

Guy extended his arm, and considered Ishtar's presence for the first time.

"Lady," said Guy. "You're naked."

"Indeed. So are you. Won't you walk this way?"

Chapter 23:
Love

"Thank you," said Ishtar, pulling the coverlet of dust around her nape.

"You mean for coming to your rescue?"

"That, too."

"Ahh."

The sleek crevasse of her cheekbone sank into his shoulder. Her fingers tickled the hair on his chest, a little wake beneath the sparkling covers. Her kiss electric silk, and bitter.

In his forty years upon the terra, Guy had experienced both abysmal lows and also more *highs* (altitudinal, astronomical, biochemical) than even the most greenly envious might have reckoned, but this—this perfect kiss—and all the incandescent delirium that had just occurred was beyond even all of that.

The wound in his abdomen was healed.

Her long, tawny leg slipped out of the linens, and formed a v across the contours of his legs. Guy's big fingers traced the flesh of her thigh, still astounded by the very solidity of her perfection.

"This is real, isn't it?" asked Guy.

"Realer than real," said the goddess.

Guy goosed her hip. Her throat emitted a flash of eternal, girly giggles, the black filaments of her hair shaking over him. He felt his body progressing through different densities, these potent, rather pleasant fluctuations, holding this goddess in his arms.

"Truly, though," she said, her palm sliding over his chest. "Thank you."

"My pleasure, then and now."

Her instep grooved along the satiny dust over his shin, the oval of her knee jutting. Her toenails glinted glossy black.

"So however did you manage to call me?" Guy asked.

"After his arrival tonight, Mr. Youngerman deigned to loan me his phone. My brother, the Lord of the Underworld, thought my maneuver pathetic, but indulged me."

"That's some terrific coverage area my provider must have."

"Divine, in that moment. Oh," she said, touching a finger to his lips. "Your face is still bruised."

"That's not a bruise," Guy said. "That's my stage paint, although I need a hell of a touch up."

"And this?" she said, tapping the side of his neck.

"Careful."

Ishtar squinted her dark eyes at the mechanism, the tiny metallic gears, clean and whirring.

"I can remedy this for you," she whispered, kissing his neck.

Guy was silent a long time, and then, smiling his big black smile, said, "No, thank you."

"Why not?"

"It's my burden to carry, and is now such a part of me. The mechanics you are studying were given to me by a remarkable man, at a great cost to himself. I owe him something. There may come a time when I can be healed, but not just yet."

"Let me."

"No."

"You're a strange and difficult man, you," she puffed.

"Aren't we all?"

"Actually, I am a woman."

A knock at the door.

"Enter," said Ishtar.

Reginald clopped into the room with a parcel. "Here are your clothes, goddess, and yours, Mr. Psycho, too. The garments you requested have been cleaned and, where necessary, mended."

"Set them over there," said Ishtar.

"Excellent, ma'am."

Reginald walked to the side of the room, where a desk held the thirteenth tablet, bathed in a gentle cone of light from a little lamp. Reginald clipped the cords of the parcel, and draped a slender black gown over a rattan crate. He slipped Guy's chalk-stripe suit and his blue oxford shirt into the various hangers of an oaken valet stand. Guy's phone and wallet, his underwear and socks, were cluttered on the shelf in the middle of the stand. His wingtips *gleamed* beneath his folded trousers.

Reginald turned around and exited backwards, his hands swinging the silent double doors closed.

Guy eyed the doors. "Where is Tammuz?" he asked.

"Right here," said the goddess, holding him tighter.

"Where is he, really?"

"It's my burden to carry," she said.

"Okay," sighed Guy.

"Your being here is the closest thing to his being here. In part, it *is* his being here."

"I have to go," Guy said.

"I know."

"Will I see you again?"

"Every time you gaze at the night sky."

"But will I ever see you again, like this?"

"Not for a very, very long time."

"Not in this lifetime?"
"Perhaps."
"Are you going to be okay?"
"Mostly."
Guy kissed her temple.
"This will be goodbye?"
"Au revoir, yes."
"In that case," said Guy, "before I go—"
"Yes—"
"We ought to do *one* more thing, while we still can."
"Yes, we must do that."

Chapter 24: Ascension

Ishtar clipped the end of the Gaultier gauze behind Guy's neck, adjusted the collar of his blue shirt.

"Thank you large," Guy said, slipping his jacket on. He gazed at himself in the mirror, his kohl darkening his eyes, his lips black. Ishtar stood behind the chair, admiring her cosmetological efforts in the glass. Her fingers slid down chalk-striped lapels, inside his jacket, inside the black elastic of his braces. His large fingers interlaced with hers, dusty against his chest. She breathed in the clean wool. She sighed.

"Now's the time," she said.

"Yes," said Guy. "Yes. Yes."

They didn't move for a long time, her kiss lingering upon his shoulder.

"The portal will be closing," she said.

"The window of opportunity," Guy said.

"Yes."

"Okay."

Guy arose and led Ishtar by the hand through the door, into the very long hallway. Candlelights danced in the brass sconces. Shadows and light alternated across their faces, their clasped hands, their footfalls on gleaming marble. Her tawny legs jutted out of her gown with each stride. Her bare feet like a sculpture.

The red EXIT sign shone faraway.

And then *closer*.

And then *close*.

Guy opened the door. Ishtar kissed his black lips, and then nudged him into the next room.

"Remember me," Ishtar said, her hand in the air.

"I wi[ll]," said Guy.

The portal contracted along its threshold, stone stretching like skin, until there was only a wall. Guy smiled, touching the wall's surface with his fingertips. He gave a throaty chuckle, and pirouetted without pain. The room was indigo, with chambers to the left and right, holding wine casks and granaries. He sank his large hands into his pockets and sauntered into the next room. He saw his strolling, elongated image in the brilliant blue water of the pool, which reminded him of Lilith. Out the final door, he saw his entourage arrayed across the precipitous stairs of the ziggurat, and whiffed the intoxicants of Chanel number 12 in the air.

Near the uppermost step, Lulu sat, her head resting on her knees, her auburn hair mussed, with the jaggedness of her geometric skirt drooping across her thighs. She heard the scratchy click of a wingtip's heel, and gazed up at the familiar silhouette inside the trapezoid of spectral white light. Her motorcycle boots sped at him, her eyes smeared with goopy mascara, a lost galaxy across her cheekbones. She collided into him with an *oomf.* The arms of her leather jacket creaked around his suit. Her fists thumped his back.

"Kiss her, you fool!" bleated Blee.

Guy squinted at the catcalls that followed. Then he smiled a big, black smile.

He clasped her hand as he descended towards the others.

"First stop," said Simone, "is the hospital."

"No[pe]," said Guy.

"But you're—" said Simone.

"Fit [as a] Stradivarius."

"How in the h—"

"Well," said Guy, "[y]ou know."

"No, I don't."

Guy smirked. Lulu let go of his hand.

"What now?" asked Aleister.

"Forthward," said Archibald, an arm around Trudy's waist. "Joey B. and Wog and Wonk are waiting up top with the bus. Let's *moose* before the fuel cells trick us up again."

Mr. Youngerman awaited them at the base of the floor level, before the huge elevator lift. A smile warped his peppery stubble, tilting his cigarette holder upward. He exhaled gray wisps through his perfect white teeth. He applauded the group as they gathered around him.

"Go[od] show?" asked Guy.

"You and your band did not disappoint."

"Good."

"I note you never performed *Windmills of Your Mind*."

"Ne[xt t]ime, T. [C.] E.," said Guy, with a black smirk.

Aleister clutched the gray flannel arm of Mr. Youngerman's jacket. "Why didn't you at least warn us, you?"

"Would you have believed me, Mr. Wrong?"

"Let'[s go]," said Guy, clapping the guitarist's shoulder.

As the elevator ascended and ascended and ascended through the tectonic strata of the earth, the musicians were stock-still, slumped, in something like a fugue state. The Postmodernaires stood with their pumps far apart, sluggish, trying to maintain their balance despite the gravitational suction of the elevator's steel floor. Enervated. Plumbs tuckered. Their gorgeous skulls a-throb. Through her clumped eyelashes, Lulu kept watch on Guy, who had slipped his huge hands into his trouser pockets. Mr. Youngerman kept his hand on the lever for a long time. He eased up on the rod, and then, the elevator crept up and up and up, until the light of the stone corridor illuminated their exhaustion.

They were shambling along towards the artifact gallery when Guy noticed a chilly passageway to another corridor, in which an infinite line of gaslight sconces diminished.

"Was thi[s] here before, T.C.E.?" Guy asked. "What's [down] that way?"

"A trifle: something called the Mystery Fun House,"® said Mr. Youngerman, "a birthday present to my grandson."

"*The* Mystery [Fun Ho]use?"

"Yes."

"From [Or]lando, Florida?"

"Quite."

"Intact?"

"Yes. Restored to its reputed acme of kitsch in 1982, in fact. We discovered that the building even has the much-rumored sixteenth chamber."

"Guy," coughed Archibald, "The Sabre Room awaits. The gig. We have to split."

"Yes, but [I'll b]e—just—a nanosecond," retorted Guy, strutting down the slope of the hallway, further and further into the dimness, until he could no longer be seen.

Thank You Large

★

A.C. Warner
Jane King
James King
Chuck Wachtel
David Lipsky
Jonathan Lethem
Darin Strauss
Risë Shifra Shamansky
Olivia Kate Cerrone
Bill Ryan
Kseniya Melnik
Jaroslav Kalfař
Richard Scott Larson
Richard Manchester
Jennifer Brachfeld Berne
Kevin Crawford
Blake Gerard
Scott Hoffman
Gila Berryman
Jason Leahy
David Foley
Carolyn Clarke
Eileen Sutton
Brooke Lewis
Andrew Crocker
Tanya Rey
David Grumblatt
Laura Schechter
Lucrecia Zappi
Sara Schneider

Miranda McLeod
Christopher Shortsleeve
Barbara Daddino
Madhubhashini Ratnayake
Vikas Mathur
Sam Schreiber
Michael Burger
Nicki Gill
Sativa January
Mark Lawley
Chad Benson
Ben Blum
Caleb Leisure
Jessie Marshall
Jonathan Padua
Caedra Scott-Flaherty
Lynn Beckenstein
Matt Peters
Tom Lucas
Leslie Carpenter
Madison Bernath
Diane Turgeon Richardson
Jeffrey Shuster
David Herst
Gary Evans
The Intoxicators
Mike Jones
Kristen Tholl-Jeancola
The Purdue Literary Awards
Bachelor Pad Magazine

About the Author

John King is the host of the world's greatest creative writing podcast, *The Drunken Odyssey*, as featured on "best of" lists by *Book Riot* and *The Millions*. He holds an MFA in fiction writing from New York University, and a doctorate in English from Purdue University. His work appears in the anthologies *15 Views of Orlando, Other Orlandos,* and *Condoms and Hot Tubs Don't Mix,* as well as in journals, such as *Gargoyle, The Newer York,* and *Painted Bride Quarterly.* He lives in a secret location in the lesser Orlando area with his wife, cat, and a cadre of robot duplicates.